EXPECTING THE
PRINCE'S BABY

EXPECTING THE PRINCE'S BABY

BY

REBECCA WINTERS

First published in Great Britain 2014
by Mills & Boon, an imprint of Harlequin (UK) Limited,
Large Print edition 2014
Eton House, 18-24 Paradise Road,
Richmond, Surrey, TW9 1SR

ISBN: 978-0-263-24099-3

Harlequin (UK) Limited's policy is to use papers that
are natural, renewable and recyclable products and made
from wood grown in sustainable forests. The logging
and manufacturing processes conform to the legal
environmental regulations of the country of origin.

Printed and bound in Great Britain
by CPI Antony Rowe, Chippenham, Wiltshire

I dedicate this book to my angelic grandmother, Alice Vivia Driggs Brown, who made my childhood a constant enchantment. She was so romantic she called the home she and my grandfather had built 'Camelot.'

CHAPTER ONE

VINCENZO DI LAURENTIS, thirty-three-year-old crown prince of the Principality of Arancia, stood before the camera on the balcony of the royal palace overlooking the gardens to officially open the April Fifteenth Lemon and Orange Festival. This was his first public appearance since the funeral of his wife, Princess Michelina, six weeks ago. He waved to the crowds that had come out en masse.

His country was nestled between the borders of France and Italy on the coast of the Mediterranean. Eighty thousand people lived in the city of the same name. The other thirty thousand made up the population that lived in the smaller towns and villages. Besides tourism, it had depended on the lemon and orange industries for centuries.

For the next two weeks the country would

celebrate the mainstay of their economy with marching bands in the streets, food fairs, floats and statuary in the parks decorated with lemons and other citrus fruit.

Vincenzo had just gotten back from a series of visits to three continents, doing business for the monarchy with other heads of state. It felt good to be with his father, King Guilio, again. On his return, he'd forgotten how beautiful Arancia could be in the spring with its orchards in full flower. He felt an air of excitement coming from the people that winter was over. As for himself, the darkness that had consumed him over the last six weeks since Michelina's death seemed to be dissipating.

Their marriage had never been a love match. Though betrothed at sixteen, they'd spent very little time together before their wedding fourteen years later. When he'd walked into their apartment earlier this afternoon, more than any other emotion, he was aware of a haunting sense of guilt for not having been able to love her the way she'd loved him.

Romantic love never grew on his part for her,

only respect and admiration for her determination to keep up the image of a happily married couple. They'd suffered through three miscarriages hoping for a child, but it hadn't happened.

His passion had never been aroused when they'd made love because he hadn't been in love with her, but he'd done his best to show her tenderness. He'd known passion with other women before he'd married Michelina. But it had only been a physical response because he was never able to give his heart, knowing he was betrothed.

Vincenzo suspected Michelina's parents had undergone the same kind of unfulfilled marriage. He knew his own parents had struggled. It was the rare occurrence when a royal couple actually achieved marital happiness. Michelina had wanted their marriage to be different, and Vincenzo had tried. But you couldn't force love. That had to spring from a source all on its own.

However there was one thing he *had* been able to do that had brought them their first real happiness as man and wife. In fact it was the only thing that had gotten him through this dark period. Just a few days before she'd died, they'd learned they were pregnant again. Only this time they'd taken the necessary steps to prevent another miscarriage.

Relieved that his last duty for today was over, he left the balcony anxious to visit the woman who'd been willing to be a gestational surrogate for them. Abby Loretto, the American girl who'd become his *friend*. Since twelve years of age she'd been living on the palace grounds with her Italian father, who was chief of security.

Vincenzo had been eighteen, with his own set of friends and a few girlfriends his own age, when Abby had arrived on the scene. Yet Abby had become the constant in the background of his life, more like a younger sister flitting in and out of his daily life. It was almost like having a sibling. In a way he felt closer to Abby than he'd ever felt to his sister, Gianna, who was six years older.

The two of them had played in the sea or the swimming pool. She was fun and bright. He could be his real self around her, able to throw off his cares and relax with her in a way he couldn't with anyone else. Because she lived on the grounds and knew the inner workings of the palace, she already had the understanding of what it was to be a royal. They didn't have to talk about it.

When his mother had died, Abby had joined him on long walks, offering comfort. When he didn't want anyone else around, he wanted her. She'd lost her mother, too, and understood what he was going through. She asked nothing from him, wanted nothing but to be his friend and share small confidences. Because they'd been in each other's lives on a continual basis, he realized it was inevitable that they'd bonded and had developed a trust.

She'd been so woven into the fabric of his life that years later, when she'd offered to be a surrogate mother for him and Michelina, it all seemed part of the same piece. His wife had liked Abby a great deal. The three of them had been in consultation for several months before the procedure had been performed. They'd worked like a team until Michelina's unexpected death.

He'd gotten used to their meetings with the doctor and the psychologist. While he'd been away on business, it had felt like years instead of weeks since he'd seen or talked to Abby. Now that she was carrying Vincenzo's son or daughter, she was his lifeline from here on out. He needed to see her and be with her.

All he could think about was getting back to make certain she and the baby were doing well. But accompanying this need was an uncomfortable sense of guilt he couldn't shake. Less than two months ago he'd lost his wife. While still in mourning over the marriage that had been less than perfect, he now found himself concentrating on another woman, who was carrying the baby he and Michelina had made.

It was only natural he cared about Abby, who'd agreed to perform this miracle. Before long he was going to be a father, all because of her! Yet with Michelina gone, it didn't seem right.

But neither was it wrong.

While he'd been traveling, he hadn't had time to dig deep into his soul, but now that he was back, he didn't know how to deal with this new emotional dilemma facing him, and he left the balcony conflicted.

Abigail Loretto, known to her friends as Abby, sat alone on the couch in her apartment at the palace, drying her hair while she was glued to the television. She'd been watching the live broadcast of Prince Vincenzo opening the fruit festival from the balcony of the palace.

Abby hadn't known he was back. Her Italian-born father, Carlo Loretto, the chief of palace security, had been so busy, he obviously hadn't had time to inform her.

She'd first met Vincenzo sixteen years earlier, when her father had been made the head of palace security. The king had brought him and his American-born wife and young daughter from the Arancian Embassy in Washington, D.C., to live in the apartment on the palace grounds. She'd been twelve to his eighteen.

Most of her teenage years had been spent

studying him, including his tall, hard-muscled physique. Instead of a film star or a famous rock star, she'd idolized Vincenzo. She'd even kept a scrapbook that followed his life, but she'd kept it hidden from her parents. Of course, that was a long time ago.

The crown prince, the most striking male Abby had ever met in her life, had many looks depending on his mood. From what she could see now, he appeared more rested since his trip.

Sometimes when he was aloof, those black eyes and furrowed brows that matched his glistening black hair made her afraid to approach him. Other times he could be charming and fun, even a tease. No one was immune from his masculine charisma. Michelina had been the most fortunate woman alive.

His picture was always on the cover of magazines and newspapers in Europe. The camera loved the handsome thirty-three-year-old son of Arancia, with his olive skin and aquiline features. Dogged by the press, he made the nightly news on television somewhere on the continent every day of the year.

The knowledge that he was home from his travels sent a wave of warmth through her body. Six weeks without seeing or talking to him about the baby had felt like an eternity. She knew he'd get in touch with her at some point. But after being away, he would have so much work to catch up on at home, it might be another week before she heard his voice on the phone.

Now that he'd left the balcony and had gone back inside the palace, the station began showing a segment of the funeral that had been televised on every channel throughout the kingdom and Europe six weeks ago.

She would never forget her father's phone call. "I have bad news. Before Vincenzo and Michelina were due to return to Arancia today, she went for an early-morning ride on her horse. Vincenzo rode with her. While she was galloping ahead of him, the horse stepped in a hole. It tossed her over end. When she hit the ground, she died on impact."

Abby froze.

Michelina was dead?

It was like déjà vu, sending Abby back to that

horrific moment when she'd learned her own mother had died.

Poor Vincenzo. He'd seen the whole thing... She couldn't stand it. "Oh, Dad—he's lost his wife. Their baby will never know its mother."

Before long she was driven to the hospital, where Dr. DeLuca had his office. "My dear Abby, what a terrible shock this has been. I'm glad your father brought you here. I'm going to keep you in the hospital overnight and possibly longer to make certain you're all right. The prince has enough pain to deal with. Knowing you're being looked after will be a great comfort to him. Excuse me while I arrange for a private room."

When he left, Abby turned to her father. "Vincenzo must be in absolute agony."

He kissed her forehead. "I know he is, but right now it's you I'm worried about. Your blood pressure is up. I plan to stay with you and will tell Signor Faustino you've caught a bad cold, but will be back to work in a few days."

"You can't stay with me here, Dad. Your place is at the palace. The king will want you there."

"Not tonight. My assistant is in charge, and Guilio wants to be there for his son. My daughter needs me, and I need you, so let that be the end of the discussion."

Her father's words had been final. Deep down she'd been glad he'd remained with her.

Abby kept watching the funeral she'd lived through once before. It was shocking to see how gaunt and shadowed Vincenzo's handsome features had been back then. His wife's death seemed to have aged him.

The most beautiful man she'd ever known in her life made a striking yet lonely figure in his mourning finery. Once again her soul shuddered to see his somber expression as he walked behind the funeral cortege toward the cathedral. He led Michelina's favorite horse from the palace stable alongside him. The chestnut mare was covered in a throw of his wife's favorite pink roses. The scene was so heart wrenching, Abby felt tears well up once again.

Behind him came the king, in his uniform of state, and his mother-in-law, dressed in a black mantilla and suit. They rode in the black-and-gold carriage with the siblings of both families. When the broadcast moved inside the cathedral, Abby listened once again to the scripture reading and remarks from the archbishop. When it was over and the bells from the cathedral rang out their mournful sound, she was once more a trembling mass of painful emotions.

"For those of you who've just tuned in, you're watching the funeral procession of Her Royal Highness Princess Michelina Cavelli, the wife of Crown Prince Vincenzo Di Laurentis of the Principality of Arancia. Earlier in the week she was killed in a tragic horse-riding accident on the grounds of the royal palace on the island kingdom of Gemelli.

"In the carriage is His Majesty Guilio Di Laurentis, King of Arancia, her father-in-law. His wife, Queen Annamaria, passed away two years ago. Seated next to him is his daughter, Princess Gianna Di Laurentis Roselli and her husband, Count Roselli of the Cinq Terres of Italy.

"Opposite them is Her Majesty Queen Bianca Cavelli, mother of Princess Michelina. Her husband, King Gregorio Cavelli of Gemelli, was recently deceased. Also seated in the royal carriage is His Royal Highness Crown Prince Valentino Cavelli of Gemelli and Prince Vitoli Cavelli, the brothers of Princess Michelina.

"On this day of great sadness for both royal houses, one has to speculate on the future of the Principality of Arancia. The world has been waiting to hear that their Royal Highnesses were expecting a child after three miscarriages, but tragically the love match between Michelina and Vincenzo ended too soon.

"Should the Princess Gianna and her husband, Count Enzio Roselli, have offspring, then their child will be third in line to—"

Abby shut off the TV with the remote and got to her feet, unable to watch any more. She shouldn't have allowed herself to live through that funeral segment a second time. Vincenzo's trip appeared to have done him some good. It was better to leave the tragic past behind and concentrate on the future.

She walked into the den to do some work at her laptop. Her dinner would be arriving shortly. Except for the occasional meal out with her best friend, Carolena, Abby normally ate in while she worked on one of her law briefs. But she had little appetite tonight.

How hard for Vincenzo to come back to the palace with no wife to greet him. His loneliness had to be exquisite and her heart ached for him.

After receiving an urgent message from his father that couldn't have come at a worse moment, Vincenzo had been given another reason to visit Abby. As he rounded the corner to her suite, he saw Angelina leaving the apartment with the dinner tray.

Angelina was Abby's personal bodyguard, hired to keep an eye on Abby, virtually waiting on her. She was the one who fed Vincenzo information on a daily basis when he couldn't be there himself. He stopped her so he could lift the cover. Abby had only eaten a small portion of her dinner. That wasn't good. He put the cover back and thanked her before knocking on the door.

"Yes, Angelina?"

He opened it and walked through until he

found Abby in the den, where he could see her at the desk working on her computer in her sweats and a cotton top. The lamp afforded the only light in the room, gilding the silvery-gold hair she must have just shampooed. He could smell the strong peach fragrance. It fell to her shoulders in a cloud.

Instead of the attorney-like persona she generally presented, she reminded Vincenzo of the lovely teenager who'd once flitted about the palace grounds on her long legs.

"Abby?"

She turned a face to him filled with the kind of sorrow he'd seen after her mother had died. "Your Highness," she whispered, obviously shocked to see him. A glint of purple showed through her tear-glazed blue eyes. She studied him for a long moment. "It's good to see you again."

Because of the extreme delicacy of their unique situation, it frustrated him that she'd addressed him that way, yet he could find no fault in her.

"Call me Vincenzo when the staff isn't around.

That's what you used to shout at me when you were running around the gardens years ago."

"Children are known to get away with murder."

"So are surrogate mothers." There was something about being with Abby. "After such a long trip, I can't tell you how much I've been looking forward to talking to you in person."

"You look like you're feeling better."

Though he appreciated her words, he wished he could say the same about her. "What's wrong? I noticed you hardly ate your dinner. Are you ill?"

"No, no. Not at all." Abby got up from the chair, rubbing the palms of her hands against the sides of womanly hips. To his chagrin the gesture drew his attention to her figure. "Please don't think that finding me in this state has anything to do with the baby."

"That relieves me, but I'm still worried about you. Anything troubling you bothers me."

She let out a sigh. "After I watched your live television appearance a little while ago, they replayed a segment of the funeral. I shouldn't have watched it." Her gaze searched his eyes. "Your suffering was so terrible back then. I can't even imagine it."

Diavolo. The media never let up. "To say I was in shock wouldn't have begun to cover my state of mind," he said.

Abby hugged her arms to her chest, once again drawing his attention to her slender waist. So far the only proof that she was pregnant came from a blood test. She studied him for a moment. "Michelina loved you so much, she was willing to do anything to give you a baby. I daresay not every husband has had that kind of love from his spouse. It's something you'll always be able to cherish."

If he could just get past his guilt over the unhappy state of their marriage. His inability to return Michelina's affection the way she'd wanted weighed him down, but he appreciated Abby's words.

Little did Abby know how right she was. In public his wife had made no secret of her affection for him and he'd tried to return it to keep up the myth of a love match. But in private Vincenzo had cared for her the way he did a friend. She'd pushed so hard at the end to try surrogacy in order to save their marriage, he'd finally agreed to consider it.

Needing to change the subject, he said, "Why don't you sit down while we talk?"

"Thank you." She did as he asked.

He subsided into another of the chairs by her desk. "How are you really feeling?"

"Fine."

"Rest assured that during my trip I insisted on being given a daily report on your progress. It always came back 'fine.'"

"It doesn't surprise me you checked. Something tells me you're a helicopter father already," she quipped.

"If you mean I'm interested to the point of driving you crazy with questions, I'm afraid I'm guilty. Since you and I have known each other from the time you were twelve, it helps me to know I can have the inside track on the guardian of my baby. Dr. DeLuca said your blood pressure went up at the time of the funeral, but it's back to normal and he promises me you're in excellent health."

Abby had a teasing look in her eye. "They say only your doctor knows for sure, but never forget he's a man and has no clue."

Laughter broke from Vincenzo's lips. It felt good to laugh. He couldn't remember the last time it had happened. "I'll bear that in mind."

"So what does the crown prince's *personal* physician have to say about the state of the expectant father?"

He smiled. "I was disgustingly healthy at my last checkup."

"That's good news for your baby, who hopes to enjoy a long, rich life with his or her daddy."

Daddy was what he'd heard Abby call her father from the beginning. The two of them had the sort of close relationship any parent would envy. Vincenzo intended to be the kind of wonderful father his own had been.

"You're veering off the subject. I told you I want the unvarnished truth about your condition," he persisted.

"Unvarnished?" she said with a sudden hint

of a smile that broke through to light up his insides. "Well. Let me see. I'm a lot sleepier lately, feel bloated and have finally been hit with the *mal di mare*."

The Italian expression for sea sickness. Trust Abby to come up with something clever. They both chuckled.

"Dr. DeLuca has given me medicine for that and says it will all pass. Then in the seventh month I'll get tired again."

"Has he been hovering as you feared?"

"Actually no. I check in at the clinic once a week before going to work. He says everything looks good and I'm right on schedule. Can you believe your baby is only one-fifth of an inch long?"

"That big?" he teased. Though it really was incredible, he found it astounding she was pregnant with a part of him. He wished he could shut off his awareness of her. Michelina's death had changed their world.

Vincenzo suspected Abby was also having to deal with the fact that the two of them were now forced to get through this pregnancy without his wife. No doubt she felt some guilt, too, because they were treading new ground neither of them could have imagined when they'd had the procedure done.

A laugh escaped her lips. "It's in the developmental stage. He gave me two identical booklets. This one is for you. Anatomy 101 for beginner fathers."

Abby...

She reached in the desk drawer and handed it to him. The title said *The Ten Stages of Pregnancy at a Glance.*

"Why ten, not nine?"

"A woman wrote it and knows these things."

He appreciated her little jokes more than she could imagine. Her normally lighthearted disposition was a balm to his soul. Vincenzo thumbed through the booklet before putting it in his pocket. When he went to bed tonight, he'd digest it.

"Thank you. Now tell me about your law cases." A safe subject that intrigued him. "Which one keeps you awake at night?"

"The Giordano case. I have a hunch someone's trying to block his initiative for political reasons."

"Run it by me."

Her arched brows lifted. "You'd be bored to tears."

"Try me." Nothing about Abby bored him.

She reached in one of the folders on her desk and handed him a printout on the case, which he perused.

As has been stated, major constraint to import into Arancia is nothing more than bureaucracy. Import certificates can take up to eight months to be released, and in some cases are not released at all. However, if the procedure is simplified, an increase of imports could particularly benefit Arancia, providing high-value high-season products.

That made even more sense to Vincenzo since talking to important exporters on his trip.

At present, the hyper/supermarket chains do not operate directly on the import market, but use the main wholesalers of oranges and lemons as intermediaries. Signor Giordano, representing the retailers, has entered the import market, thus changing some long-established import partnerships. He's following a different strategy, based on higher competition, initial entry fees and spot purchases, thus bringing more revenue to Arancia.

Vincenzo knew instinctively that Signor Giordano was really on to something.

Signor Masala, representing the importers, is trying to block this new initiative. He has favored cooperative producers and established medium-to long-term contracts, without requiring any entry fee. The figures included in this brief show a clear difference in revenue, favoring Signor Giordano's plan.

I'm filing this brief to the court to demonstrate that these high-quality products for fast-track approval would benefit the econ-

*omy and unfortunately are not unavailable
in the country at the present time.*

Vincenzo handed her back the paper. Her knowledge and grasp of their country's economic problems impressed him no end. He cocked his head. "Giuseppe Masala has a following and is known as a hard hitter on the trade commission."

Abby's brows met in a delicate frown. "Obviously he's from the old school. Signor Giordano's ideas are new and innovative. He's worked up statistics that show Arancia could increase its imports of fuel, motor vehicles, raw materials, chemicals, electronic devices and food by a big margin. His chart with historical data proves his ideas will work.

"I'd like to see him get his fast-track idea passed, but the lobby against it is powerful. Signor Masala's attorney is stalling to get back to me with an answer."

She had him fascinated. "So what's your next strategy?"

Abby put the paper back in the folder. "I'm

taking him to court to show cause. But the docket is full and it could be awhile."

"Who's the judge?"

"Mascotti."

The judge was a good friend of Vincenzo's father. Keeping that in mind, he said, "Go on fighting the good fight, Abby. I have faith in you and know you'll get there."

"Your optimism means a lot to me."

She was friendly, yet kept their relationship at a professional distance the way she'd always done. To his dismay he discovered he wanted more, in different surroundings where they could be casual and spend time talking together like they used to. Her suite wasn't the right place.

Her bodyguard already knew he'd stopped by to see her and would know how long he stayed. He wanted to trust Angelina, but you never knew who your enemies were. Vincenzo's father had taught him that early on. So it was back to the business at hand. "The doctor's office faxed me a schedule of your appointments. I understand you're due for your eight weeks' checkup on Friday, May 1." She nodded. "I plan to join you at the clinic and have arranged for us to meet with the psychologist for our first session afterward."

"You mean you'll have time?" She looked surprised.

"I've done a lot of business since we last saw each other and have reported in to the king. At this juncture I'm due some time off and am ready to get serious about my duties as a father-in-waiting."

Laughter bubbled out of her. "You're very funny at times, Vincenzo."

No one had ever accused him of that except Abby. He hated bringing the fun to an end, but he needed to discuss more serious matters with her that couldn't be put off before he left.

"Your mention of the funeral reminds me of how compassionate you are, and how much you cared for Michelina. I've wanted to tell you why we decided against your attending the funeral."

She moistened her lips nervously. "My father already explained. Naturally, none of us wanted the slightest hint of gossip to mar your life in any way. Just between us, let me tell you how much I liked and admired Michelina. I've missed my daily talks with her and mourn her loss."

He felt her sincerity. "She cared for you, too."

"I—I wish there'd been a way to take your pain away—" her voice faltered "—but there wasn't. Only time can heal those wounds."

"Which is something you know all about, after losing your mother."

"I'll admit it was a bad time for Dad and me, but we got through it. There's no burning pain anymore."

When he'd seen Carlo Loretto's agony after losing his wife, Vincenzo had come to realize how lucky they'd been to know real love. Abby had grown up knowing her parents had been lovers in the true sense of the word. Obviously she could be forgiven for believing he and Michelina had that kind of marriage. *A marriage that had physically ended at the very moment there was new hope for them.*

"Did your father explain why I haven't phoned you in all these weeks?"

"Yes. Though you and Michelina had told me we could call each other back and forth if problems arose, Dad and I talked about that too. We decided it will be better if you and I always go through your personal assistant, Marcello."

"As do I."

It would definitely be better, Vincenzo mused. She understood everything. With Michelina gone, no unexplained private calls to him from Abby meant no calls to be traced by someone out to stir up trouble. They'd entered forbidden territory after going through with the surrogacy.

Vincenzo had to hope the gossip mill within the palace wouldn't get to the point that he could no longer trust in the staff's loyalty. But he knew it had happened in every royal house, no matter the measures taken, and so did she.

"I mustn't keep you, but before I go, I have a favor to ask."

"Anything."

"Michelina's mother and brothers flew in for the festival." It was an excuse for what the queen really wanted. "She would like to meet with you and me in the state drawing room at nine in the morning."

His concern over having to meet with his mother-in-law had less to do with the argument Michelina and the queen had gotten into before the fatal accident, and much more to do with the fact that he hadn't been able to love her daughter the way she'd loved him. He was filled with guilt and dreaded this audience for Abby's sake. But his mother-in-law had to be faced, and she had refused to be put off. "Your father will clear it with your boss so he'll understand why you'll be a little late for work."

"That's fine."

It wouldn't be fine, but he would be in the room to protect her. "Then I'll say good-night."

She nodded. "Welcome home, Vincenzo, and *buonanotte*." Another smile broke out on her lovely face.

"Sogni d'oro."

CHAPTER TWO

THE PRINCE'S FINAL words, "sweet dreams," stayed with her all night. Seeing him again had caused an adrenaline rush she couldn't shut off. She awakened earlier than usual to get ready, knowing Michelina's mother would ask a lot of questions.

Abby always dressed up for work. Since the law firm of Faustino, Ruggeri, Duomo and Tonelli catered to a higher-class clientele, Signor Faustino, the senior partner, had impressed upon her and everyone else who worked there the need to look fashionable. Though her heart wasn't in it this morning, she took her antinausea pill with breakfast, then forced herself to go through the motions.

Everyone knew she was the daughter of the chief of security for the palace, so no one questioned the royal limo bringing her to and from work. Except for her boss and Carolena, her coworkers were clueless about Abby's specific situation. That's the way things needed to remain until she took a leave of absence.

After the delivery, the palace would issue a formal statement that a surrogate mother had successfully carried the baby of their Royal Highnesses, the new heir who would be second in line to the throne. At that time Abby would disappear. But it wouldn't be for a while.

Vincenzo had been a part of her life for so long, she couldn't imagine the time coming when she'd no longer see him. Once the baby was born, she would live in another part of the city and get on with her life as a full-time attorney. How strange that was going to be.

From the time she'd moved here with her family, he'd been around to show her everything the tourists never got to see. He'd taken her horseback riding on the grounds, or let her come with him when he took out his small sailboat. Vincenzo had taught her seamanship. There was nothing she loved more than sitting out in the middle of the sea while they fished and ate sweets from the palace kitchen. He had the run of the place and let her be his shadow.

Abby's friends from school had come over to her parents' apartment, and sometimes she'd gone to their houses. But she much preferred being with Vincenzo and had never missed an opportunity to tag along. Unlike the big brothers of a couple of her friends who didn't want the younger girls around, Vincenzo had always seemed to enjoy her company and invited her to accompany him when he had free time.

Memories flooded her mind as she walked over to the closet and pulled out one of her favorite Paoli dresses. When Abby had gone shopping with Carolena, they'd both agreed this one had the most luscious yellow print design on the body of the dress.

The tiny beige print on the capped sleeves and hem formed the contrast. Part of the beige print also drew the material that made tucks at the waist. Her friend had cried that it was stunning on Abby, with her silvery-blond hair color. Abby decided to wear it while she still could.

The way she was growing, she would need to buy loose-fitting clothes this weekend.

After arranging her hair back in a simple low chignon with three pins, she put on her makeup, slipped on matching yellow shoes and started out of the bedroom. But she only made it to the hallway with her bone-colored handbag when her landline rang. Presuming it was her father calling to see how she was doing, she walked into the den to pick up and say hello.

"Signorina Loretto? This is Marcello. You are wanted in the king's drawing room. Are you ready?"

Her hand gripped the receiver tighter. It sounded urgent. During the night she'd worried about this meeting. It was only natural Michelina's mother would want to meet the woman who would be giving birth to her grandchild. But something about the look in Vincenzo's eyes had given her a sinking feeling in the pit of her stomach.

"Yes. I'll be right there."

"Then I'll inform His Highness, and meet you in the main corridor."

"Thank you."

Because of Vincenzo, Abby was familiar with every part of the palace except the royal apartments. He'd taken her to the main drawing room, where the king met with heads of state, several times. Vincenzo had gotten a kick out of watching her reaction as he related stories about foreign dignitaries that weren't public knowledge.

But her smile faded as she made her way across the magnificent edifice to meet Michelina's mother. She knew the queen was grieving. Marcello met her in the main hallway. "Follow me."

They went down the hall past frescoes and paintings, to another section where they turned a corner. She spied the country's flag draped outside an ornate pair of floor-to-ceiling doors. Marcello knocked on one of the panels and was told to enter. He opened the door, indicating she should go in.

The tall vaulted ceiling of the room was a living museum to the history of Arancia, and had known centuries of French and Italian rulers.

But Abby's gaze fell on Vincenzo, who was wearing a somber midnight-blue suit. Opposite him sat Michelina's stylish sixty-five-year-old mother, who was brunette like her late daughter. She'd dressed in black, with a matching cloche hat, and sat on one of the brocade chairs.

"Come all the way in, Signorina Loretto. I'd like you to meet my mother-in-law, Her Majesty the Queen of Gemelli." Abby knew Gemelli—another citrus-producing country—was an island kingdom off the eastern coast of Sicily, facing the Ionian Sea.

She moved toward them and curtsied the way she'd been taught as a child after coming to the palace. "Your Majesty. It's a great honor, but my heart has been bleeding for you and the prince. I cared for your daughter very much."

The matriarch's eyes were a darker brown than Michelina's, more snapping. She gave what passed for a nod before Vincenzo told Abby to be seated on the love seat on the other side of the coffee table. Once she was comfortable, he said, "If you recall, Michelina and I flew to

Gemelli so she could tell the queen we were pregnant."

"Yes."

"To my surprise, the unexpected nature of our news came as a great shock to my mother-in-law, since my wife hadn't informed her of our decision to use a surrogate."

What?

"You mean your daughter never told you what she and the prince were contemplating?"

"No," came the answer through wooden lips.

Aghast, Abby averted her eyes, not knowing what to think. "I'm so sorry, Your Majesty."

"We're all sorry, because the queen and Michelina argued," Vincenzo explained. "Unfortunately before they could talk again, the accident happened. The queen would like to take this opportunity to hear from the woman who has dared to go against nature to perform a service for which she gets nothing in return."

CHAPTER THREE

ABBY REELED.

For Vincenzo to put it so bluntly meant he and his mother-in-law had exchanged harsh if not painfully bitter words. But he was a realist and had decided the only thing to do was meet this situation head-on. He expected Abby to handle it because of their long-standing friendship over the years.

"You haven't answered my question, Signorina Loretto."

At the queen's staccato voice, Abby struggled to catch her breath and remain calm. No wonder she'd felt tension from him last night when he'd brought up this morning's meeting. Michelina's omission when it came to her mother had put a pall over an event that was helping Vincenzo to get up in the morning.

He was counting on Abby being able to deal

with his mother-in-law. She refused to let him down even if it killed her. More time passed while she formulated what to say before focusing on the queen.

"If I had a daughter who came to me in the same situation, I would ask her exactly the same question. In my case, I've done it for one reason only. Perhaps you didn't know that the prince rescued me from certain death when I was seventeen. I lost my mother in that same sailboat accident. Before I was swept to shore by the wind, I'd lost consciousness.

"When the prince found me, I was close to death but didn't know it." Abby's eyes glazed over with unshed tears. "If you could have heard the way my father wept after he discovered I'd been found and brought back to the living, you would realize what a miracle had happened that day, all because of the prince's quick thinking and intervention.

"From that time on, my father and I have felt the deepest gratitude to the prince. Over the years I've pondered many times how to pay the prince back for preventing what could have been an all-out catastrophe for my father."

The lines on the queen's face deepened, revealing her sorrow. Whether she was too immersed in her own grief to hear what Abby was saying, Abby didn't know.

"The prince and princess were the perfect couple," Abby continued. "When I heard that the princess had had a third miscarriage, it wounded me for their sake. They deserved happiness. Before Christmas I learned through my father that Dr. DeLuca had suggested a way for them to achieve their dream of a family."

Abby fought to prevent tears from falling. "After years of wishing there was something I could do, I realized that if I could qualify as a candidate, I could carry their child for them. You'll never know the joy it gave me at the thought of doing something so special for them. When I told my father what I wanted to do, he was surprised at first, and yet he supported my decision, too, otherwise he would never have approved."

She took a shuddering breath. "That's the reason I'm doing this. A life for a life. What I'm going to get out of this is pure happiness to see the baby the prince and princess fought so hard for. When the doctor puts the baby in the prince's arms, Michelina will live on in their child, and the child will forever be a part of King Guilio and his wife, and a part of you and your husband, Your Majesty."

The queen's hands trembled on the arms of the chair. "You have no comprehension of what it's like to be a mother. How old are you?"

"I'm twenty-eight and it's true I've never been married or had a child. But I won't be its mother in the way you mean. I'm only supplying a safe haven for the baby until it's born. Yes, I'll go through the aches and pains of pregnancy, but I view this as a sacred trust."

Her features hardened. "You call this sacred?"

"I do. During my screening process, I met a dozen different parents and their surrogates who'd gone through the experience and now have beautiful children. They were all over-joyed and agreed it's a special partnership be-tween them and God."

For the first time, the queen looked away.

"The prince is a full partner in this. He and the princess discussed it many times. He knows what she wanted and I'll cooperate in every way. If you have suggestions, I'll welcome them with all my heart."

Quiet reigned.

Realizing there was nothing more to say, Abby glanced at Vincenzo, waiting for him to dismiss her.

He read her mind with ease. "I'm aware the limo is waiting to drive you to your office."

"Yes, Your Highness."

At those words Michelina's mother lifted her head. "You intend to work?" She sounded shocked.

"I do. I am passionate about my career as an attorney. After the delivery, I will have my own life to lead and need to continue planning for it."

Vincenzo leaned forward. "She'll stop work when the time is right."

"Where will you live after the baby's born?" The pointed question told Abby exactly where the queen's thoughts had gone.

Nowhere near the prince.

She couldn't blame the older woman for that. How could Michelina's mother not suspect the worst? Her fears preyed on Abby's guilt, which was deepening because she'd found herself missing Vincenzo more than she should have while he'd been away. He shouldn't have been on her mind so much, but she couldn't seem to turn off her thoughts. Not when the baby growing inside her was a constant reminder of him.

For weeks now she'd played games of *what if?* during the night when she couldn't sleep. What if the baby were hers and Vincenzo's? What would he or she look like? Where would they create a nursery in the palace? When would they go shopping for a crib and all the things necessary? She wanted to make a special baby quilt and start a scrapbook.

But then she'd break out in a cold sweat of guilt and sit up in the bed, berating herself for having any of these thoughts. Michelina's death might have changed everything, but this royal baby still wasn't Abby's!

How could she even entertain such thoughts

when Michelina had trusted her so implicitly? It was such a betrayal of the trust and regard the two women had for each other. They'd made a contract as binding as a blood oath. The second the baby was born, her job as surrogate would no longer be required and she'd return to her old life.

But Abby was aghast to discover that Michelina's death had thrown her into an abyss of fresh guilt. She needed to talk to the psychologist about finding strategies to cope with this new situation or go crazy.

Queen Bianca had asked her a question and was waiting for an answer.

"I plan to buy my own home in another part of the city in the same building as a friend of mine. My contract with the prince and princess includes living at the palace, and that ends the moment the baby is delivered."

Vincenzo's eyes narrowed on her face. "What friend?"

That was probably the only thing about her plans the three of them hadn't discussed over the last few months.

"You've heard me speak of Carolena Baretti and know she's my best friend, who works at the same law firm with me. We went through law school together at the University of Arancia before taking the bar."

If a woman could look gutted, the queen did. "This whole situation is unnatural."

"Not unnatural, Your Majesty, just different. Your daughter wanted a baby badly enough to think it all through and agree to it. I hope the day will come when you're reconciled to that decision."

"That day will never come," the older woman declared in an imperious voice. "I was thrilled each time she informed me she was pregnant and I suffered with her through each miscarriage. But I will never view surrogacy as ethically acceptable."

"But it's a gestational surrogacy," Abby argued quietly. "Dr. DeLuca says that several thousand women around the globe are gestational surrogates and it's becoming preferable to going with traditional surrogacy, because it ensures the genetic link to both parents. Think how many lives can be changed. Surely you can see what a miracle it is."

"Nevertheless, it's outside tradition. It interferes with a natural process in violation of God's will."

"Then how do you explain this world that God created, and all the new technology that helps people like your daughter and Vincenzo realize their dream to have a family?"

"It doesn't need an explanation. It's a form of adultery, because you are the third party outside their marriage. Some people regard that it could result in incest of a sort."

Tortured by her words, Abby exchanged an agonized glance with Vincenzo. "What do you mean?"

"As the priest reminded me, their child might one day marry another of *your* children. While there would be no genetic relationship, the two children would be siblings, after a fashion."

Naturally Abby hoped to marry one day and have children of her own, but never in a million years would she have jumped to such an improbable conclusion. By now Vincenzo's features had turned to granite.

"There's also the question of whether or not you'll be entitled to an inheritance and are actually out for one."

Abby was stunned. "When the prince saved my life, he gave me an inheritance more precious than anything earthly. If any money is involved, it's the one hundred and fifty thousand dollars or more the prince has paid the doctors and the hospital for this procedure to be done." She could feel herself getting worked up, but she couldn't stop.

"I've been given all the compensation I could ever wish for by being allowed to live here in the palace, where my every want and need is taken care of. I'm so sorry this situation has caused you so much grief. I can see you two need to discuss this further, alone. I must leave for the office."

Abby eyed the prince, silently asking him to please help her to go before the queen grew any more upset. He got the message and stood to his full imposing height, signaling she could stand.

"Thank you for joining us," he murmured. "Whatever my mother-in-law's reaction, it's too late for talk because you're pregnant with Michelina's and my child. Let's say no more. I promise that when the queen is presented with her first grandchild, she'll forget all these concerns."

The queen flashed him a look of disdain that wounded Abby. She couldn't walk out of here with everything so ugly and not say a few last words.

"It's been my privilege to meet you, Your Majesty. Michelina used to talk about you all the time. She loved you very much and was looking forward to you helping her through these coming months. I hope you know that. If you ever want to talk to me again, please call me. I don't have a mother anymore and would like to hear any advice you have to help me get through this."

It was getting harder and harder to clap with one hand and the prince knew it.

"Again, let me say how sorry I am about your loss. She was so lovely and accomplished. I have two of her watercolors hanging on the wall of my apartment. Everyone will miss her terribly, especially this baby.

"But thankfully it will have its grandmother to tell him or her all the things only you know about their mother."

The queen stared at Abby through dim eyes.

Abby could feel her pain. "Goodbye for now." She curtsied once more. Her gaze clung to Vincenzo's for a few seconds before she turned on her low-heeled sandals and left the room. The limo would be waiting for her. Though she wanted to run, she forced herself to stay in control so she wouldn't fall and do something to hurt herself.

The queen had put Abby on trial. No wonder Vincenzo's wife had been frightened to approach her mother with such an unconventional idea. Only now was Abby beginning to understand how desperate *and* courageous Michelina had been to consider allowing a third party to enter into the most intimate aspect of all their lives. Facing the queen had to be one of the worst moments Abby had ever known.

But this had to be an even more nightmarish experience for Vincenzo. Here he was trying to deal with his wife's death while at the same time having to defend the decision he and Michelina had made to use a surrogate. He had to be suffering guilt of his own.

Abby blamed no one for this, but she felt Vincenzo's pain. How he was going to get through this latest crisis, she couldn't imagine. Probably by working. That was how *she* planned to survive.

Twenty minutes later Abby entered the neoclassical building that housed her law firm and walked straight back to Carolena's office. Her friend was a patent attorney and had become as close to Abby as a sister. Unfortunately she was at court, so they'd have to talk later.

Both Carolena and Abby had been hired by the well-known Arancian law firm after they'd graduated. Abby had been thrilled when they'd both been taken on a year ago. She had planned for this career from her junior-high days, and had been hired not only for her specialty in international trade law, but because she was conversant in French, English, Italian and Mentonasc.

Since the Mentonasc dialect—somewhere between Nicard and a dialect of Ligurian, a Gallo-Romance language spoken in Northern Italy—was currently spoken by about 10 percent of the population living in Arancia and its border areas, it gave her an edge over other applicants for the position, which required her particular linguistic expertise.

Abby's parents had cleverly directed her studies from a very young age. Thanks to them her abilities had taken her to the head of the class. However, this morning Abby's mind wasn't on her latest cases.

She felt disturbed by the revelation that Michelina had kept her mother in the dark about one of the most important events in her life. Abby had done her research. Since the death of King Gregorio, Queen Bianca become the ruler of Gemelli and was known to be rigid and difficult. Abby had felt her disapproval and didn't envy Vincenzo's task of winning his mother-in-law over.

Hopefully something Abby had said would sink in and soften her heart. At the moment, Abby's own heart was breaking for all of them.

Six hours later, Abby finished dictating some memos to Bernardo and left the building for the limo. But when she walked outside, she noticed the palace secret service cars had parked both in front of and behind the limo. One of the security men got out of the front and opened the rear door for her. What was going on?

As she climbed inside and saw who was sitting there waiting for her—in sunglasses and a silky claret-colored sport shirt and cream trousers—the blood started to hammer in her ears.

"Vincenzo—"

His name slipped out by accident, proving to her more and more that he filled her conscious and unconscious mind.

The tremor in Abby's voice made its way to every cell of Vincenzo's body. After she'd bared her soul to his mother-in-law that morning, he'd realized not only at what price she'd sacrificed herself to make their dreams of a baby a reality, but he'd been flooded with memories of that day when she'd lost her mother.

Abby had been a great swimmer and handled herself well in the sea. As some of his friends had pointed out years ago when they'd seen her in the water offshore, she wasn't a woman yet, but she showed all the promise.

By the time she'd turned seventeen, he'd found himself looking at her a lot more than he should have. She was one of those natural-blond American girls with classic features, noted for their long, gorgeous legs. At that point in time Vincenzo had already been betrothed to Michelina. Since the marriage wouldn't be for at least another ten years, he'd had the freedom to date the women who attracted him.

Abby had been too young, of course, but pleasing to the eye. She'd turned into a very beautiful girl who was studious, intelligent and spoke Italian like a native. He enjoyed every moment he spent with her; her enthusiasm for everything surprised and entertained him.

But even if he hadn't been betrothed, Abby had been off-limits to Vincenzo for more reasons than her young age or the fact that she wasn't a princess. Her parents had become close friends with Vincenzo's parents. That was a special friendship that demanded total respect.

Though her periwinkle-blue eyes always seemed to smile at him with interest when they chanced upon each other, there was an invisible boundary between them she recognized, too. Neither of them ever crossed it until the day of the squall…

As Abby had told Queen Bianca earlier, she and her mother, Holly, had been out in a small sailboat off the coast when the storm struck. Nothing could come on as rapidly and give so little time for preparation as did a white squall.

Vincenzo had been in his father's office before lunch discussing a duty he needed to carry out when they'd noticed the darkening sky. A cloudburst had descended, making the day feel like night. They hadn't seen a storm this ferocious in years and felt sorry for anyone who'd been caught in it.

While they were commenting on the fierceness of the wind, a call came through informing the king that the Loretto sailboat was missing from its slip. Someone thought they had seen Signora Loretto and her daughter out sailing earlier, but they hadn't come back in yet. Several boats were already out there looking for them.

Abby—

Vincenzo was aghast. *She* was out there?

The sweet girl who'd always been there for him was battling this storm with her mother, alone?

Fear like Vincenzo had never known before attacked his insides and he broke out in a cold sweat. "I've got to find them!"

"Wait, son! Let the coast guard deal with it!"

But he'd already reached the door and dashed from the room. Driven by fear, he raced through the palace. Once outside, he ran to the dock, where a group of men huddled. He grabbed one of them to come with him and they took off in his cruiser to face a churning sea.

The other man kept in radio contact with the rescue boats. Within a minute they heard that the sailboat had been spotted. Vincenzo headed toward the cited coordinates, oblivious to the elements.

The rescue boats were already on the scene as Vincenzo's cruiser came close to the sail-boat. It was tossing like a cork, but he couldn't see anyone on board. "Have they already been rescued?"

"Signora Loretto was found floating unconscious in the water wearing her life preserver, but there's no sign of her daughter yet," replied his companion.

Vincenzo's heart almost failed him.

Abby had drowned?

It was as though his whole life passed before him. She *couldn't* have drowned! He couldn't lose her! Not his Abby...

"We've got to look for her! She knows to wear a life jacket. The wind will have pushed her body through the water. We're going to follow it. You steer while I search."

"It's too dangerous for you, Your Highness!"

"Danger be damned! Don't you understand?" he shouted. "There's a seventeen-year-old girl out there who needs help!"

"Tell me where to go."

He studied the direction of the wind. "Along the coastline near the caves!" Vincenzo knew this coastline like the back of his hand. When a low pressure over the Mediterranean approached the coast from the southeast, the weather could change quickly for the worse and its clear sky change to an east wind. If Abby had been knocked unconscious, too, she could have been swept into one of the caves further up the coast.

When they reached the opening of the largest cave, Vincenzo dove in and swam through to the three hidden grottoes, where he'd been many times with his friends. In the second one, his heart had leaped when he saw Abby's body floating lifelessly, like her mother's. Quickly he'd caught hold of her and swum her out to the boat, where he took off her life jacket and began giving her mouth-to-mouth resuscitation. At first there was no response. Her face was a pinched white. Though terrified she was too far gone, he kept up the CPR.

At the last second there came sounds of life, and her eyelids fluttered. He turned her on her side while she coughed and threw up water.

"That's it, my precious Abby. Get rid of it."

When she'd finished, she looked up at him, dazed. "Vincenzo?"

"*Sì,*" he'd murmured in relief. "You were in a storm, but I found you in one of the grottoes and you're all right now."

Abby blinked. "My mother?" she cried frantically. "Where is she?"

"With your father." It wasn't a lie, but since he didn't know the whole truth of her condition, he kept quiet.

"Thank God." Her eyes searched his. "I could have died in there. You saved my life," she whispered in awe. In a totally unexpected gesture, she'd thrown her arms around his neck and clung to him.

"Thank God," he'd whispered back and found himself rocking her in his arms while she sobbed.

Vincenzo had never felt that close to another human being in his life. She'd felt so right in his arms. When they took her to the hospital and she learned her mother had died of a blow from the mast, she'd flung herself into his arms once more.

That was the moment when he knew Abby meant more to him that he could put into words. Their relationship changed that day. His feelings for her ran much deeper than he'd realized. To imagine his life without her was anathema to him.

She'd been too inconsolable for him to do anything but let her pour out her pain and love for her mother. His only desire had been to comfort her. He'd held her for a long time because her father, overcome with grief, had to be sedated.

In front of the queen today, they'd both relived that moment. Abby's outpouring of her soul had endeared her to him in such a profound way, he could hardly find expression. Though he knew it was wrong, he'd decided to break one of his own rules and pick her up from work.

Bianca had put Abby through a torturous session. Despite his guilt in seeking her out for a reason that wasn't a medical necessity, he couldn't let it go until he'd seen for himself that she was all right.

"I came to find out how well you survived the day."

The picture of her in that yellow dress when she'd walked in the room had made an indelible impression of femininity and sophistication in his mind. Bianca couldn't have helped but notice how lovely she was, along with her moving sincerity. It hadn't surprised him his mother-in-law had been so quiet after Abby had left the room to go to work.

"My worry has been for you." She sat down opposite him and fastened her seat belt. "For me, work is the great panacea. But it's evident the queen has been in absolute agony."

"She's flown back to Gemelli with a lot to think about."

"The poor thing. We have to hope she'll let

go of her preconceived beliefs so she can enjoy this special time."

There was a sweetness in Abby that touched Vincenzo's heart. "You're the one I'm concerned about. It hurts me that you no longer have your mother to confide in." Until now he hadn't thought about how alone Abby must feel. Bianca's castigations had been like a dagger plunged into her, bringing out his protective instincts.

She flicked him a glance. "But I have my father, and I have you and the doctor. Who better than all of you to comfort me when I need it?" Except that Vincenzo wanted to do more than comfort her, God forgive him.

He held her gaze. "I'm sorry if anything the queen said has upset you, but I promise everything's going to be all right in time."

"I believe that, too. Did she say anything else?"

"No, but her son Valentino and I are good friends." When he'd gone with the queen and his brothers-in-law to visit Michelina's grave once, they'd eaten lunch before he'd accompanied them to their jet. "He's promised to keep in close touch. Now let's change the subject."

"You're taking too great a risk, Your Highness. We mustn't be seen out together like this."

"The limo protects us." Even as he said it, he was trying to tamp down his guilt over pressuring her when it was obvious she was afraid to be seen with him. He ought to be worried about that, too, but something had come over him.

"Please, Your Highness. The fact that there are so many security men will cause the locals to speculate about who is so important, driving around in the crowded streets. Have the car turn around and take me back to the office."

"It's too late for that." Vincenzo had no intention of letting her go yet.

"After my audience with the queen, surely you understand my fears."

"After the way she went after you, I have my own fears where you're concerned. You didn't deserve that and I want to make it up to you."

CHAPTER FOUR

"WE'RE GOING IN the wrong direction to the palace."

Vincenzo ignored Abby's comment. "Last night you didn't eat a full meal. This evening I intend to remedy that and take you to a very special place for dinner to celebrate the Lemon and Orange Festival. Don't worry," he said when he saw her eyes grow anxious. "We'll be arriving via a private entrance to a private dining room where my own people will be serving us. All you have to do is enjoy a meal free of caffeine and alcohol, with salt in moderation."

She kneaded her hands. "I know why you're doing this, Vincenzo, but it isn't necessary."

"Has being pregnant made you a mind reader?"

For once she couldn't tell if he was having

fun with her or if her comment had irked him. "I only meant—"

"You only meant that you don't expect any special favors from me," he preempted her. "Tell me something I don't already know."

"I've annoyed you. I'm sorry."

"Abby—we need to have a little talk. Because of the sacrifice you've made for me and Michelina, any social life you would normally enjoy has been cut off until the baby's born. At this time in your life you should be out having a good time. I have no doubt there are any number of men who pass through your office wanting a relationship with you. Certainly I don't need to tell you that you're a very beautiful woman. My brother-in-law shared as much with me earlier."

"I've never met Michelina's brother."

"But he saw you this morning after you left the drawing room for the limo."

That was news to Abby. Vincenzo's words had shaken her. "Thank you for the compliment."

"Now you sound vexed with me."

"I'm not!"

"Good. Then try to understand that our relationship isn't one-sided, with me reaping all the benefits while you lie around like a beached whale, barefoot and pregnant, as you Americans tend to say."

Abby burst into laughter.

"I'm glad you think that's funny. We're making progress."

No one could be more amusing than Vincenzo when he revealed this exciting side of his nature. "I can't believe you've ever heard those expressions."

"I graduated in California Girls 101 during my vacation one summer in San Diego."

She rolled her eyes. "*That* school. I don't doubt it." She knew he'd traveled a lot in his twenties. "I guess you didn't need a booklet for the class."

He grinned, revealing a gorgeous white smile. "And the tuition was free. Why do you think most men congregate there when they get the chance?"

"Isn't it interesting that most women congregate in Arancia and Italy to attend Mediterranean Gods 101? They don't need booklets, either."

Vincenzo let go with a belly laugh that resonated throughout the interior of the limo. "You must be dynamite in the courtroom."

"Why don't you come up and see me some time?" she said in her best Mae West impersonation. *Why didn't he come to her apartment and stay...* It was a wicked thought, but she couldn't help it. The other night she hadn't wanted him to leave.

The corner of his mouth lifted. "Who were you imitating just now?"

"Someone you'd never know. She was in American films years ago. My mother loved her old movies."

"Tell me her name."

"I'll give you a hint. They named inflatable life jackets after her in the Second World War. If you still can't think of it, I'll do better and have a DVD sent to you so you can see for yourself."

"We'll watch it together."

No. They wouldn't watch it together. They'd done enough of that when she was much younger. He had his own theater in the palace, where she'd seen a lot of films and eaten marzipan with him. But that time was long gone and this idea of his had to be stopped right now. She was having too much fun and needed his company too much.

Thankfully they'd left the Promenade d'Or along the coast and were following a winding road up the hillsides above the city. In another minute they rounded a curve and pulled up to, of all things, a funicular railway.

Vincenzo got out of the limo and came around to help her. Together with some of his security people, they got on and sat on one of the benches. He told her to buckle up before it started climbing the steep mountain.

"There's a lovely little restaurant two kilometers higher that overlooks the Mediterranean. While we eat, we'll watch the festival fireworks being set off in town."

Once Abby was settled, Vincenzo had to talk to one of his security men, leaving her alone with her thoughts for a second. During her teenage years she'd had ridiculous daydreams about being alone with him, but none of them could match the wonder of such an evening. Without question this was the most thrilling moment in Abby's life.

However, there was one problem with reality intruding on this beautiful dream. While he was trying to give her a special night out to make up for her being denied a social life at present, Abby could never forget she was carrying the child he and Michelina had made. The wife he'd adored was gone, leaving him desolate, just like her father.

She remembered the night of Michelina's funeral, when she'd wandered out onto the patio of her apartment, not knowing where to go with her pain. Before her was the amazing sight of dozens of sailboats and yachts anchored offshore from up and down the Riviera with Arancian flags flying at half-mast in the breeze to pay respect to the prince.

While she stood there, her cell phone had rung, causing her to jump. She hurried inside to check the caller ID, hardly able to see through the tears.

"Carolena?" she'd cried after clicking on.

"Abby? When the announcer started speculating on the future of the monarchy, I had to call and see if you're all right."

She breathed in deeply. "Yes," she'd murmured, wiping the moisture off her cheeks with her hand.

"No, you're not. I don't know how you're handling this."

"Truthfully, not very well."

"Talk to me. I know you told me you can't leave the palace until tomorrow and I can't come over there today, so the phone will have to do. Have you even talked to Vincenzo since the accident?"

"Yes. He came for a minute last evening, worried about my welfare, if you can imagine."

"Actually, I can. To know you're carrying his child is probably the only thing keeping him from going under. I never witnessed anything more touching in my life than the sight of the horse covered in her favorite flowers walking alongside that incredible-looking man. Already I've seen one of the tabloids out in the kiosk bearing the headline The Prince of Every Woman's Dreams in Mourning."

Abby had closed her eyes tightly. "The media will make a circus of this." She could hear it all now: *Who will be the next princess? Will she be foreign? Will he wait a year, or will he break with tradition and take a new bride in the next few months?* Abby had a question of her own: *How will the next woman he chooses feel about the surrogacy situation?* All those thoughts and more had bombarded her.

"You really shouldn't be alone."

"All I have to do is get through tonight, Carolena. Tomorrow I can start living a normal life."

Now, seven weeks later, here Abby was with the prince of every woman's dreams, riding to the top of the mountain. But there was nothing normal about his life or hers. When she and her father had gone through all the *what if*s before she'd made her decision to be a surrogate, the idea of either Michelina or Vincenzo dying had only been mentioned in passing. But she couldn't have imagined anything so horrible and never thought about it again.

"Shall we go in?" sounded the deep, velvety male voice next to her.

"Oh—yes!" Abby had been so immersed in thought she hadn't realized they'd arrived. Night had fallen during their journey here. Vincenzo led her off the funicular and walked her through a hallway to another set of doors. They opened onto a terrace with a candlelit table and flowers set for two.

A small gasp of pleasure escaped her lips when she realized she was looking out over the same view she could see from her own patio at the palace. But they were much higher up, so she could take in the whole city of Arancia alive with lights for the nightly festival celebration.

"What an incredible vista."

"I agree," he murmured as he helped her to sit. Of course it was an accident that his hand brushed her shoulder, but she felt his touch as if she'd just come in contact with an electric current. This was so wrong; she was terrified.

Grape juice from the surrounding vineyard came first, followed by hors d'oeuvres and then a luscious rack of lamb and fresh green peas from the restaurant's garden. Abby knew the chef had prepared food to the prince's specifications.

She ate everything. "This meal is fabulous!"

His black eyes smiled at her. "Tonight you have an appetite. That's good. We'll have to do this more often."

No, no, no.

"If I were to eat here every night, I'd be as big as that whale you referred to earlier."

He chuckled. "You think?"

"I know."

While Abby enjoyed the house's lemon tart specialty for dessert, Vincenzo drank coffee. "Mind if I ask you a personal question?"

How personal? She was on dangerous ground, fearing he could see right through her, to her chaotic innermost thoughts. "What would you like to know?"

"Has there been an important man in your life? And if so, why didn't you marry him?"

Yes. I'm looking at him.

Heat filled her cheeks. "I had my share of boyfriends, but by college I got serious about my studies. Law school doesn't leave time for much of a social life when you're clerking for a judge who expects you to put in one hundred and twenty hours a week."

"Sounds like one of my normal days," he remarked. She knew he wasn't kidding. "You and I never discussed this before, but I'm curious about something. Didn't you ever want to be a mother to your own child first?"

Abby stifled her moan. If he only knew how during her teenage years she'd dreamed about being married to him and having his baby. Since that time, history had been made and she was carrying his baby in real life. But it wasn't hers and that dream had come with a price. How could she be feeling like this when he was forbidden to her?

"Well—" She swallowed hard. "The desire to be a mother has always been rooted in me. I've never doubted my ability to be a good one. Despite the fact that Mother died early, I had a charmed and happy childhood. She was a wonderful mom. Warm and charming. Funny. Still, I never saw raising a child as my only goal.

"I'd always envisioned motherhood as the result of a loving relationship with a man, like my parents had. Carolena has told me many times that it's just an excuse because no man has ever lived up to my father. She said the umbilical cord should have been cut years ago. With hindsight I think she's probably right, but there's no one like him."

In truth, there was no one like Vincenzo and never would be. *He* was the reason she hadn't been able to get interested in another man.

"Your father has been a lucky man to have inspired such fierce love from his wife and daughter."

The comment sounded mournful. "Michelina loved you the same way."

"Yes."

"So will your child."

His eyes grew veiled without him saying anything.

The fireworks had started, lighting up the night sky in a barrage of colors, but she couldn't appreciate the display because of a certain tension between them that hadn't been there earlier. She was walking such a tightrope around him, her body was a mass of nerves.

"Maybe coming out to dinner wasn't a very good idea for you, Your Highness."

"What happened to *Vincenzo?*"

Again she had the feeling she'd angered him, the last thing she wanted to do. But it was imperative she keep emotional distance from him. "You're still mourning your wife. I appreciate this evening more than you know, but it's too soon for you to be out doing the things you used to do with her." *And too hard on me.*

She wiped her mouth with the napkin. "When was the last time you brought her here? Do you want to talk about it?"

That dark, remote expression he could get had returned. "Michelina never came here with me."

She swallowed hard. "I see." She wondered why. "Nevertheless, being out on a night like this has to bring back memories."

His fingers ran over the stem of the wineglass that was still full. "Today as I opened the festival, you could feel spring in the air. You can feel it tonight. It calls for a new beginning." His gaze swerved to hers, piercing through to her insides. "You and I are together on a journey that neither of us has ever taken. I want to put the past behind us and enjoy the future that is opening up."

"With your baby to be born soon, it will be a glorious future."

"There are a few months to go yet, months you should be able to enjoy. I want to help you. How does that sound?"

It sounded as though he didn't want to be reminded of his wife again because it hurt him too much and he needed a diversion. Naturally, he did, but Abby couldn't fill that need! She didn't dare.

"I'm already having a wonderful time enjoying this meal with you. Thank you for a very memorable evening."

"You're welcome. I want us to enjoy more."

"We can't, Vincenzo. The people close to you will notice and there will be gossip. If I've angered you again, I'm sorry."

Silence followed her remarks. They watched the fireworks for a while longer before leaving.

The ride down the mountain was much faster than the ride up. It was much like the sensation when Dr. DeLuca had said, "Congratulations, Signorina Loretto. The blood test we did revealed the presence of the HCG hormone. You're pregnant!"

Abby hadn't believed it. Even though she'd wanted to be a surrogate mother and had done everything possible to make it happen, for the doctor to tell her the procedure had worked was like the first time she rode the Ferris wheel at a theme park. The bar had locked her in the chair, filling her with excitement. Then the wheel had turned and lifted her high in the air. That was the way she felt now, high in the air over Arancia. She didn't know if she wanted this descent to continue, but it was too late to get off. She had to go with it and just hang on. Only this time she wasn't on the Ferris wheel or the funicular and this ride would continue for the next thirty-odd weeks.

Abby hadn't been able to tell anyone about her pregnancy except Carolena. But she knew she could trust her best friend with her life, and that news hadn't been something she could keep to herself on that day of all days.

When she went to work on the day she'd found out she was pregnant, Abby visited with her gorgeous, fashionable Italian friend, who stopped traffic when she stepped outside. Carolena had worn her chestnut hair on top of her head in a loose knot. Though she didn't need glasses, she put on a pair with large frames to give her a more professional appearance.

She looked up when she saw Abby and smiled. "*Fantastico!* I've been needing a break from the Bonelli case."

"I'm so happy you said that because I've got something to tell you I can't hold in any longer. If I don't talk to you about it, I'll go crazy." She closed and locked the door behind her before sitting down in the chair opposite the desk.

"This has to be serious. You looked flushed. Have you settled the Giordano case already? Shall we break out the champagne?"

"Don't I wish! No, this has nothing to do with

the law." She moved restlessly in the leather chair. In fact there'd be no champagne for her for the next nine months. "What I say to you can't ever leave this room."

Carolena's smile faded before she crossed herself.

Abby leaned forward. "I'm going to have a baby," she whispered.

Her friend's stunned expression said it all before she removed her glasses and walked around the desk in her fabulous designer sling-back high heels to hunker down in front of her. She shook her head. "Who?" was all she could manage to say.

The question was a legitimate one. Though Abby had been asked out by quite a few men since joining the firm, she hadn't accepted any dates. No on-site romances for her. Besides, she wanted to make her place in the firm and that meant studying when she wasn't in the office so she could stay on top of every case.

"Their Royal Highnesses."

Carolena's beautifully shaped dark brows met together in a frown. "You mean…as in…"

"Prince Vincenzo and Princess Michelina."

There was a palpable silence in the room. Then, "Abby—"

"I realize it's a lot to swallow."

A look of deep concern broke out on Carolena's expressive face. "But you—"

"I know what you're going to say," she broke in hurriedly. "It's true that I'll always love him for saving me from drowning, but that was eleven years ago when I was seventeen. Since then he has married and they've suffered through three miscarriages. The doctor suggested they look for a gestational surrogate mother for them."

"What?"

"His logic made total sense. Gestational surrogacy, unlike adoption, would allow both Vincenzo and Michelina to be genetically related to their child. Even better, they would be involved in the baby's conception and throughout the pregnancy, so they'd feel a total part of the whole experience."

"But you can't be a surrogate because you've never had a baby before."

"There are a few exceptions, and I'm one of them."

Carolena put a hand on Abby's arm. "So you just nominated yourself for the position without any thought of what it would really mean and threw yourself into the ring?" She sounded aghast at the idea.

Abby had hoped for a happier response from her friend. "Of course not. But I wasn't able to stop thinking about it. I even dreamed about it. The answer of how to repay him for saving my life came to me like a revelation. *A life for a life.*"

"Oh, Abby—despite the fact that you push men away, you're such a romantic! What if midway through the pregnancy you become deathly ill and it ruins your life? I can't even imagine how awful that would be."

"Nothing's going to happen to me. I've always been healthy as a horse. I want to give them this gift. I didn't make the decision lightly. Though I had a crush on him from the time I was twelve, it had nothing to do with reality and I got over it after I found out he was already betrothed to Michelina."

Those famous last words she'd thrown out so recklessly had a choke hold on Abby now. She adored him, but had to hide her feelings if it killed her.

By the time she and Vincenzo had climbed in the limousine, she realized her due date was coming closer. In one regard she wanted it to get here as quickly as possible. But in another, she needed to hug the precious months left to her, because when it was over, she wouldn't see Vincenzo again. She couldn't bear the thought.

When Abby's eight-week checkup was over, Dr. DeLuca showed her into another consulting room, where she saw Vincenzo talking with the psychologist, Dr. Greco. Both men stood when she entered. The prince topped him by at least three inches.

Her vital signs had been in the normal range during her exam, but she doubted they were now. Vincenzo possessed an aura that had never made him look more princely. He wore a cream-colored suit with a silky brown sport shirt, the picture of royal affluence and casual sophistication no other man could pull off with the same elegance.

The balding doctor winked at her. "How is Signorina Loretto today, besides being pregnant?" She liked him a lot because he had a great sense of humor.

"Heavier."

Both men chuckled before they all sat down.

The doctor lounged back in his chair. "You do have a certain…how do you say it in English? A certain bloom?"

"That's as good an English term as I know of to cover what's really obvious. I actually prefer it to the Italian term *grassoccia*."

"No one would ever accuse you of looking chubby, my dear."

Vincenzo's black eyes had been playing over her and were smiling by now. The way he looked at her turned her insides to mush. She felt frumpy in the new maternity clothes she'd bought. This morning she'd chosen to wear a khaki skirt with an elastic waist and a short-sleeved black linen blouse she left loose fitting.

The outfit was dressy enough, yet comfortable for work. Her little belly had definitely enlarged, but Carolena said you wouldn't know it with the blouse hanging over the waist.

Dr. Greco leaned forward with a more serious expression. "A fundamental change in both your lives has occurred since you learned the embryo transfer was successful. We have a lot to talk about. One moment while I scroll to the notes I took the last time we were together."

Abby avoided looking at Vincenzo. She didn't know if she could discuss some of the things bothering her in front of the doctor. Up to the moment of Michelina's death, when she'd been through a grueling screening with so many tests, hormones and shots and felt like a scientific experiment, she'd thought she'd arrived at the second part of her journey. The first part had been the months of preparation leading up to that moment.

Abby recalled the smiles on the faces of the hopeful royal couple, yet she knew of their uncertainty that made them feel vulnerable. The three of them had seen the embryo in the incubator just before the transfer.

It was perfect and had been inserted in exactly the right place. The reproductive endocrinologist hugged Michelina and tears fell from her eyes. Vincenzo's eyes had misted over, too. Seeing their reaction, Abby's face had grown wet from moisture. The moment had been indescribable. From that time on, the four of them were a team working for the same goal.

For the eleven days while she'd waited for news one way or the other, Abby had tried to push away any thoughts of failure. She wanted to be an unwavering, constant source of encouragement and support.

When the shock that she was pregnant had worn off and she realized she was carrying their child, it didn't matter to her at all that the little baby growing inside of her wasn't genetically hers. Abby only felt supreme happiness for the couple who'd suffered too many miscarriages.

Especially *their* baby, who would one day be heir to the throne of the Principality of Arancia.

Vincenzo's older sister, Gianna, was married to a count and lived in Italy. They hadn't had children yet. The honor of doing this service of love for the crown prince and his wife superseded any other considerations Abby might have had.

But her world had exploded when she'd learned of Michelina's sudden death. The news sent her on a third journey outside her universe of experience. Vincenzo had been tossed into that black void, too.

"Before you came in, Vincenzo told me about the meeting with you and his mother-in-law," said the doctor. "He knows she made you very uncomfortable and feels you should talk about it rather than keep it bottled up."

She bit her lip. "*Uncomfortable* isn't the right word. Though I had no idea the queen had such strong moral, ethical and religious reservations against it, my overall feeling was one of sadness for Vincenzo."

"He feels it goes deeper than that."

Abby glanced at Vincenzo. "In what way?"

The doctor nodded to him. "Go ahead."

Vincenzo had an alarming way of eyeing her

frankly. "When we went out to dinner the other night, you weren't your usual self. Why was that?"

She prayed the blood wouldn't run to her face. "Months ago we decided to be as discreet as possible. Since your wife's death I've feared people would see us together and come to the wrong conclusion. But you already know that."

"The queen put that fear in you without coming right out and saying it, didn't she?"

This was a moment for brutal honesty. "Yes."

"Abby—our situation has changed, but my intention to go through this pregnancy with you is stronger than ever. You shouldn't have to feel alone in this. I intend to do all the things Michelina would have done with you and provide companionship. I don't want you to be afraid, even if people start to gossip about us."

She shuddered. "Your mother-in-law is terrified of scandal. I could see it in her eyes. It's evident that's why Michelina was afraid to tell her the truth. The other morning I sensed the queen's shock once she heard you'd saved my life, and that I'd lived on the palace grounds since the age of twelve.

"It wouldn't be much of a stretch for her to believe that not only am I after an inheritance, but that I'm after you. I even feared she believes I've been your mistress and that the baby isn't her grandchild."

"I *knew* that's what you were worried about the other night," Vincenzo whispered.

"I wish Michelina had talked to her mother before the decision was made to choose a surrogate, Your Highness."

"So do I. It grieves me that my wife was always intimidated by her and couldn't admit she hadn't told her mother first, but what's done is done and there's no going back."

Abby was in turmoil. "Vincenzo and Michelina have broken new royal ground with my help, Dr. Greco. Unfortunately it's ground that Queen Bianca isn't able to condone. I'm half-afraid she's going to demand that the pregnancy be…terminated." The thought sickened Abby to the point that she broke out in a cold sweat.

"Never," Vincenzo bit out fiercely. "She

wouldn't go that far, not even in her mind, but she's going to have to deal with it since the time's coming when people will know you're the surrogate."

The doctor looked at both of them with concern. "Vincenzo is right. I think it's good you've already felt the fire by dealing with Michelina's mother first. To my knowledge no other royal couple in the known world has undergone the same procedure. The situation involving the two of you is an unprecedented case, but a wonderful one since it means preserving the royal line."

"Here's my dilemma." Vincenzo spoke up once more. "Before Michelina's death I'd planned to keep a lower profile around you, Abby, but that's impossible now and I can't have you feeling guilty. Of course we'll try to be careful, but only within reason. Otherwise I'll be worried about the stress on you and the baby."

"Vincenzo makes a valid point, Abby," the doctor inserted.

She lowered her head. "I know he's right. The moment I decided to go through with this, I realized it would be a risk, but I felt helping them was worth it. But with the princess gone…"

"Yes. She's gone, but you still need to keep that noble goal uppermost in your mind. One day soon you'll be free to live your own life again and the gossip will be a nine-day wonder. Do you have any other issues you'd like to discuss with me in this session?"

Yes. How did she keep her emotional distance from Vincenzo when he'd just stated that he intended to be fully involved with her?

"I can't think of any right now."

"You, Vincenzo?"

He shook his dark, handsome head. "Thank you for meeting with us. I'm sure we'll be talking to you again." Vincenzo got to his feet. "Abby needs to get back to work and so do I."

The three of them shook hands before they left his office and walked out of the building to the limousine. Abby's office wasn't that far away from the hospital. When the limo pulled up in front of the entrance, Vincenzo reached over to open the door for her.

"Have you made plans for the evening, Abby?"

"Yes," she lied. "Carolena and I are going to enjoy the festival before it ends."

"Good. Be careful not to tire yourself out."

She didn't dare ask him what he was doing tonight. It was none of her business. How on earth was she going to get through seven more months of this?

Vincenzo watched until Abby hurried inside before he closed the door and told his driver to head for the palace. For the moment he had an important meeting with the minister of agriculture. That would keep him occupied until Abby got off work.

If she'd been telling the truth and had plans with her friend, then he was in for a night he'd rather not think about. But she didn't make a good liar. He'd known her too long. He had the strongest hunch she would go straight back to the palace after work and dig into one of her law cases. If he was right—and he would find out later—he'd take her for a walk along the surf.

Incredible to believe that the girl he'd saved from drowning eleven years ago had become a gorgeous woman in every sense of the word, *and* was carrying his child. Even though Michelina had been the biological mother, Abby was now the birth mother.

Though there'd been other candidates, the second he'd heard that Abby was one of them, his mind was made up on the spot. Because she'd always lived on the grounds and they'd developed a special bond, he knew her in all those important little ways you could never know about another person without having had that advantage.

Abby was smart, kind, polite, thoughtful, intelligent, fun. In fact, he knew that he would never have gone through with the surrogacy process if she hadn't been on the list. Michelina had been determined to go through with it because she was desperate to fix their marriage. After her incessant pleading, his guilt finally caused him to cave about turning to the procedure for the answer.

No matter how hard they'd tried, theirs had been a joyless union they'd undergone to perform a duty imposed by being born into royalty. He'd driven himself with work, she with her hobbies and horseback riding. Part of each month she spent time in Gemelli, riding with her friends. They had been counting on a child to bring happiness to their lives.

Thanks to the pregnant woman who'd just left the limo, his baby would be born in November. It would have been the miracle baby his arranged marriage had needed to survive. Now that he was alone, he needed that miracle more than ever. His eyes closed tightly. But he needed Abby, too…

CHAPTER FIVE

"ABBY?"

"Yes, Bernardo?"

"You just received a message from Judge Mascotti's court. Your case for Signor Giordano has been put on the docket for June 4."

"So soon?"

"It surprised me, too."

"Wonderful. I'll call my client."

That kind of good news helped her get through the rest of the afternoon. At five-thirty Abby said good-night to Carolena, who was going out on a date with a friend of her cousin, and hurried out to the limousine. She needed to let go of any unwanted feeling of guilt for lying to Vincenzo over her plans for the evening.

Once she reached the palace, she walked to her suite with its exposure to the water. In her opinion, her new temporary home, set in the heart of the coastal city, was the jewel in the crown of the Principality of Arancia.

At a much younger age, Vincenzo had shown her around most of the palace and she'd adored the older parts. Nine weeks ago she'd been moved from her dad's apartment to the palace and installed in one of the renovated fourteenth-century rooms, with every convenience she could imagine. It thrilled her that Vincenzo had remembered this one was her favorite.

The maid had told her he'd had it filled with fresh flowers, just for her. When she heard those words Abby's eyes smarted, but she didn't dare let the tears come in front of the staff.

Her bedroom had a coffered ceiling and was painted in white with lemon walls up to the moldings. The color matched the lemons of the trees clumped with the orange trees in the gardens below. This paradise would be hers until the baby was born. Vincenzo had told her she had the run of the palace and grounds until then.

She'd marveled at his generosity, but then, he'd always been generous. Years earlier, when she'd mentioned that she wanted a bike to get around sometimes and hoped her parents would get her one for Christmas, he'd provided one for her the very next day.

They did a lot of bike riding on the extensive grounds and had races. He let her win sometimes. She wondered what the doctor would say if she went for a bike ride now. If he gave her permission, would Vincenzo join her? It was a heady thought, one she needed to squelch.

After a snack, Abby decided to take a swim in the pool at the back of the palace and told Angelina she wouldn't want dinner until later. She was supposed to get some exercise every day and preferred swimming to anything else in order to unwind.

Once she'd put her hair in a braid and pinned it to the top of her head, she threw on a beach robe over her bikini and headed out wearing thonged sandals. When she reached the patio, she noticed Piero Gabberino pulling weeds in the flower bed.

"Ciao, Piero!"

"*Ehi,* Abby!"

The chief gardener's nice-looking son, who would be getting married shortly, had always been friendly with her. They'd known each other for several years and usually chatted for a while when they saw each other.

When she'd found out he was going to college, she took an interest in his plans. Three weeks ago Saturday she'd invited him to bring his fiancée and have lunch with her on the patio. The young couple were so excited about the coming marriage, it was fun to be around them.

"Only a week until the wedding, right?"

He grinned. *"Sì."*

She removed her robe and got in the pool. The water felt good. She swam to the side so she could talk to Piero. "I'm very happy for you. Thank you for the invitation. I plan to come to the church to see you married." Both she and her father had been invited, but she didn't know if her dad would be able to take the time off.

Piero walked over to the edge of the pool and hunkered down. "Thank you again for the lunch. Isabella always wanted to come to the palace and see where I work."

"It's a beautiful place because you and your father's crew keep the grounds in exquisite condition."

"*Grazie.*"

"Aren't you working a little late this evening?"

"I had classes all day today."

"I know what that's like. Have you and Isabella found an apartment yet?"

"Two days ago. One day soon you will have to come over for dinner."

"That would be lovely."

"*Buonasera,* Piero!"

At the sound of Vincenzo's deep voice, Abby's heart thudded. She flung herself around in the water at the same time Piero got to his feet.

"Your Highness! It's good to see you again. Welcome home."

"Thank you. You look well."

"So do you. May I take this moment now to tell you how sorry I am about the princess. We've all been very sad."

"I appreciate those kind words."

As long as Abby had known Vincenzo, he'd almost always gone swimming in the sea in the evenings and did his early-morning workouts in the pool. Now she'd been caught in the act of lying.

He looked incredible in a pair of black swim trunks with a towel thrown around his broad shoulders. Mediterranean Gods 101 could have used him for their model.

Vincenzo eyed both of them. "Don't let me disturb the two of you."

"I was just leaving. *Scusi,* Your Highness." He gave a slight bow to Vincenzo and walked back to the plot of flowers to get his things before leaving the patio.

Abby shoved off for the other side of the rectangular pool while she thought up an excuse why she hadn't gone out with Carolena. She heard a splash and in seconds Vincenzo's dark head emerged from the surface of the water next to her.

His unreadable black eyes trapped hers. "Why did you tell me you had plans with Carolena when it's obvious you wanted to rush home after work to be with Piero? My apologies if I interrupted something between the two of you.

You both looked like you were enjoying your-selves."

Her heart fluttered out of rhythm. Coming from any other man, Abby could be forgiven for thinking he was jealous. But that was absurd.

"Before work was over, Carolena told me she'd been lined up with her cousin's friend, so we decided to do something tomorrow evening instead." That was partially a lie, too, but she would turn it into a truth if at all possible.

She could hear his brilliant wheels turning. "Have you and Piero been friends long?"

"Quite a few years. He speaks Mentonasc and has been a great teacher for me. I, in turn, have been coaching him in one of his first-year law classes, but he doesn't really need help."

His black brows lifted in surprise. "He's going to be an attorney?"

"That's been his hope since he was young. He has been influenced by his father to get a good education. Some kind of business law, probably. I've been helping him review appellate court decisions and analyze the judges' reasoning and findings. He's very bright."

Vincenzo looked stunned. "I'm impressed."

"Six months ago he got himself engaged and is going to be getting married next week. I met his fiancée the other day and we had lunch together out here. They've invited me to the wedding next week. I'm thrilled for them."

Vincenzo raked a hand through his wet black hair. "Apparently a lot has been going on around here, under my nose, that I've known nothing about."

"You have so much to do running the country. How could you possibly know everything? Don't forget I've lived on the grounds for years and am friends with everyone employed here. When I was young the gardeners helped me find my mom's cat, who went out prowling at night and never wanted to come home."

Vincenzo's smile was back, reminding her of what a sensational-looking male he was.

"Sometimes they brought me a tiny wounded animal or a bird with a broken wing to tend. Piero's father used to call me 'little nurse.'"

His gaze played over her features and hair. She saw a tenderness in his eyes she'd never noticed before. "All the same, I should have been more observant."

"Need I remind you that your royal nose has much greater worries, like dealing with your country's welfare?" He chuckled. "The word *multitask* could have been coined on your work ethic alone. Don't you remember the dead starling I found and you helped me plan a funeral for it?"

He nodded. "You were so broken up about it, I had to do something."

"It was a wonderful funeral." Her voice started to tremble. "You even said a prayer. I'll never forget. You said that some angels watched over the birds, but if they couldn't save them, then they helped take away the child's sorrow."

His black brows lifted. "I said that?"

"Yes. It was a great comfort to me." *You've always been a great comfort to me.*

"Your praise is misplaced, but like any man I admit to enjoying a little flattery."

"It's the truth. I have a scrapbook to prove it." Her confession was out before she could prevent it. Feeling herself go crimson, she did a somersault and swam to the deep end of the pool to cool down. When she came up gasping for air, he was right there, without a sign of being winded. If her heart didn't stop racing pretty soon, she was afraid she'd pass out. "Haven't you learned it's impolite to race a woman with a handicap, and win?"

His eyes grew shuttered. "Haven't you learned it's not nice to tease and then run?"

Touché.

"When am I going to see this scrapbook?"

Making a split-second decision, she said, "I plan to send it to you when your child is christened." She couldn't help searching his striking features for a moment. "The pictures showing you and your wife will be especially precious. I can promise that he or she will treasure it."

Abby heard his sharp intake of breath. "How long have you been making it?"

"Since soon after we arrived from the States."

"Clear back then?"

"Don't you know every girl grows up dreaming about palaces and princes and princesses? But my dream became real. I decided I would record everything so that one day I could show my own little girl or boy that I once lived a fairy-tale life.

"But now that you're going to have a little girl or boy, *they* should be the one in possession of it. The story of your life will mean everything in the world to them. If they're like me when I was young and poured over my parents' picture albums for hours and hours, they'll do the same thing."

Vincenzo was dumbfounded. Evening had crept over the palace, bringing out the purity of her bone structure, but he saw more than that. An inward beauty that radiated. It was that same innocent beauty he'd seen in her teens, but the added years had turned her into a breathtaking woman.

He wondered what she'd say if he told her that....

Of course he couldn't, but something earth-shattering was happening to him. As if he was coming awake from a hundred-year sleep. Vincenzo was starting to come alive from a different source, with feelings and emotions completely new to him. Not even his guilt could suppress them.

"I'm looking forward to that day, Abby."

"You're not the only one." But she said it with a charming smile. He liked her hair up in a braid. She wore it in all kinds of ways, each style intriguing.

"Shall we swim a couple of laps before we have dinner? When I talked to Angelina and she told me you hadn't eaten yet, I arranged for us to be served out here on the patio." While she was forming an answer he said, "I promise to let you set the pace."

"Thank you for taking pity on me." On that note, she started for the other side of the pool.

Vincenzo swam beside her, loving this alone time with her. There was no tension. A feeling of contentment stole through him. At the moment he was feeling guilty for *not* feeling guilty. He asked himself if he would feel this way if she weren't pregnant, but it wasn't a fair question. With Michelina gone, he naturally felt more protective toward Abby, who no longer had a female mentor to turn to for support.

To his surprise, he'd been disturbed to find her talking and laughing with Piero. *Why* had he felt that way? Was it the helicopter father coming out in him, as she'd suggested? Vincenzo frowned. Was he already becoming possessive?

Her comment about never finding a man who measured up to her father had been on his mind since they'd eaten at the mountain restaurant. He wondered if she'd ever been intimate with any of her boyfriends. If the answer was no, then in one respect he understood his mother-in-law's remark about the pregnancy being unnatural.

Just how would Vincenzo feel when Abby did get married, knowing she'd carried his child for nine months before she'd known another man? When she did get married one day—he had no doubt about that—how would the man she loved feel to know she'd given birth to Vincenzo's baby? Would that man feel robbed in some way?

His thoughts kept going. What if Vincenzo

wanted to marry a woman who'd already given birth through surrogacy? It would mean she'd already gone through a whole history with some other man and his wife. Would that change the way he felt about her?

The more he pondered the subject, the more he couldn't answer his own questions.

While he succeeded in tying himself up in knots, Abby climbed the steps to leave the pool. For a moment he caught a side view of her lovely body. His heart clapped with force to see her stomach wasn't quite as flat as he remembered, but at this stage you wouldn't know she was pregnant. Dr. DeLuca had said that since this was her first pregnancy, it might be awhile.

That didn't matter. *Vincenzo knew.*

The day Abby had given him that pamphlet, he'd studied it and learned she would probably start showing by twelve weeks. Michelina had lost their three babies by that point, so he'd never seen his wife looking pregnant.

His excitement grew to imagine Abby in another month. Since he wasn't the most patient man, the waiting was going to be hard on him.

And what about her? She was the one going through the travail that brought a woman close to death. Her patience had to be infinite.

He found himself asking the same question as the queen: What *did* Abby get out of this?

Vincenzo had listened to her explanation many times, but right now he was in a different place than he'd been at Christmas when they'd talked about surrogacy as an answer. His focus hadn't been the same back then. Now that he was no longer desperate for himself and Michelina, he had a hard time imagining this remarkable woman, who could have any man she wanted, being willing to go through this.

How did any surrogate mother who wasn't already a mother or who had never given birth leave the hospital and go back to her old life without experiencing changes, psychologically and emotionally? He could understand why it was illegal in many parts of the world for someone like Abby. He and Michelina must have been so blinded by their own unhappiness that they'd agreed to let Abby go through with this.

Though they'd discussed everything before

the procedure, nothing had seemed quite real back then. Those same questions were haunting him now in new, profound ways. A fresh wave of guilt attacked him. He needed to explore his feelings in depth with Dr. Greco, because he was concerned for Abby's welfare. She was having to put off being with other men until the baby was born. That meant putting off any possible marriage. To his dismay, the thought of her getting married brought him no joy. What was wrong with him?

Abby put on her white beach robe over her green bikini and they sat down to dinner. "This cantaloupe is so sweet I can't believe it."

"I hear it's especially good for you."

"You're spoiling me, you know."

He gripped his water glass tighter. "That's the idea. You're doing something no one should expect you to do."

A wounded look entered her eyes. "I didn't *have* to do anything, Vincenzo. It was my choice."

"But you've never been pregnant before. My wife and I were entirely selfish."

Michelina because she'd wanted so much to have a child. Vincenzo because he'd wanted Abby to be the woman if they did decide to go through with it. The perfect storm…

After drinking the rest of his water, he darted her another glance. "Though I know you would never admit it to me, you've probably regretted your decision every day since the procedure was done."

She put down her fork. "Stop it, Vincenzo!" It pleased him she'd said his name again.

"You know the reason I did this and you couldn't be more wrong about my feelings now. Why don't we take Dr. Greco's advice and drop all the guilt? Let's agree that though this is an unprecedented case, it's a wonderful one that's going to give you a son or daughter. We need to keep that goal foremost in our minds."

Vincenzo sucked in a deep breath. "So be it! But I have to tell you that you're the bravest, most courageous soul I've ever known."

"You mean after you. Let's not forget *you*

were the one who dove into that cave looking for my body during the most ferocious storm I'd ever seen after moving to Arancia. It wasn't the men in the coast guard who'd performed that deed.

"Their first duty was to protect you. Instead they let you risk your life to save me. If Father hadn't been so devastated over losing Mother at the time, those men would have faced severe penalties, so I'd say we're equal."

There was no one like Abby when her back got up. "All right." He lifted his water glass.

"Truce?"

She did likewise. "Truce." They touched glasses.

After she drank a little and put her glass on the table, he could tell there was something else on her mind. "What were you going to say?"

"How did you know?" she asked, bemused.

"A feeling."

She was quiet for a moment. "Today a minor miracle occurred when I received word that Judge Mascotti is going to hear the Giordano case in less than a month. I was expecting it to be six at the earliest." She eyed him with blue eyes that sparkled with purple glints in the candlelight. "Who do you suppose was responsible?"

"I have no idea," he said in a deadpan voice.

"Liar." No one had ever dared call him that, but then, no one was like Abby. "I'm very grateful, you know. It's my biggest case so far with the firm."

"You've got a good one. My bet is on you to win it in the end."

"Please don't hold your breath."

He smiled. "In my line of work I'm used to doing it. Don't forget I have to face our constitutional assembly on a weekly basis, and they're *all* stars." Laughter bubbled out of her, but he noticed she'd drawn her beach robe closer around her. "It's cooling off, Abby. Since you have another workday tomorrow, I mustn't keep you up any longer."

She got up from the table before he could help her. "I've enjoyed the company and dinner very much. After your good deed in getting my law case heard sooner, I have to hope my side will prevail. *Buonanotte,* Vincenzo."

Her disappearance left him at a loss. As he walked swiftly to his apartment, Vincenzo phoned Marcello. "My mail included an invitation for the wedding of Luigi Gabberino's son. Can you give me the particulars?"

"Momento." Vincenzo headed for the bathroom to take a shower while he waited.

"Friday at four o'clock, San Pietro Church."

"Grazie. Put that date on my calendar. I intend to go."

"I'm afraid there's a conflict. You'll be in a meeting with the education minister at that time."

"I'll cut it short."

"Bene, Your Highness."

On Friday Abby left work at three-thirty in order to get to the church and be seated by four. She'd worn a new designer dress in Dresden-blue silk to the office. The top of the square-necked two-piece outfit shot with silver threads draped below the waistline. The sleeves were stylishly ruched above the elbow. On her feet she wore low-heeled silver sandals.

She'd caught her hair back in a twist with pins. Once she'd bid her latest client goodbye, she retouched her makeup before pulling the new floppy broad-brimmed hat with the silvery-blue rose from her closet. After putting it on, she grabbed her silver bag and left the office with a trail of colleagues gawking in her wake. Carolena had been with her when she'd bought the outfit, and now gave her the thumbs-up.

Outside the building she heard whistles and shouts of *bellissima* from the ever-appreciative male population of Arancia. She chuckled. What a gorgeous, sunny day for a wedding! There was a delightful breeze off the Mediterranean.

The limo wound through the streets until it came to a piazza fronting the church of San Pietro, where she was let out. Abby followed a group of people inside and found a seat in the assembled crowd of friends and extended family. She recognized several employees from the palace, and of course Piero's immediately family.

Before the Mass began, heads turned as a side door opened. When she saw Vincenzo enter surrounded by his bodyguards, she started to feel light-headed. The exquisitely groomed prince of Arancia wore a dove-gray suit. He was heartbreakingly handsome and took her breath away, along with everyone else's.

He sat off to the side. Piero's parents had to feel so honored. This was the second time Vincenzo had gone out of his way to perform a service that hadn't been on his agenda—the first, of course, being a word put in Judge Mascotti's ear to hasten Abby's court case hearing.

The prince was an amazingly thoughtful man. She'd worked around a lot of men. No man of her acquaintance could touch him. Abby knew deep in her heart he was so grateful for her being willing to carry his baby, there wasn't enough he could do for her. It was something she would have to get used to. When he dedicated himself to a project, he went all out.

For the next hour Abby sat there eyeing him with covert glances while Piero and his bride took their vows. When the service was over,

Vincenzo went out the side exit while she followed the crowd outside to the piazza to give the radiant couple a hug. But when she was ready to walk to her limousine, one of the security men touched her elbow.

"Signorina Loretto? If you would come with me, please."

With heart thumping, she followed him around the side of the church to another limousine, where she knew Vincenzo was waiting inside. The breeze was a little stronger now. As she started to climb in, she had to put her hand on her hat to keep it in place. At the same time, her skirt rode up her thighs. She fought madly with her other hand to push it down.

Vincenzo's dark eyes, filled with male admiration, missed nothing in the process, causing her to get a suffocating feeling in her chest. The hint of a smile hovered at the corners of his compelling mouth. After she sat down opposite him, he handed her the silver bag she'd accidentally dropped.

"Thank you," she said in a feverish whisper.

"Anyone could be forgiven for thinking *you*

are the bride. That color is very becoming on you. We can't let such a stunning outfit go to waste. What is your pleasure?"

Her pleasure… She didn't dare think about that, let alone take him up on his offer.

"To be honest, it's been a long day. I'm anxious to get back to the palace and put my feet up. If that sounds ungracious, I don't mean for it to be."

"Then that's what we'll do." He let his driver know and the limo started to move out to the street. His arms rested along the back of the seat. He looked relaxed. "I enjoyed the wedding."

"So did I. Piero was beaming. I know he was a happy groom, but your presence made it the red-letter day in all their lives. That was very kind of you, Vincenzo."

"I have you to thank for reminding me of my duty. Now that it's over, we'll concentrate on taking care of you. When we get back to the palace we'll have dinner in your apartment and watch a movie I ordered."

Ordered? Her pulse raced. "I'm sure you have other things to do."

His black eyes glinted with a strange light. "Not tonight. It will feel good to relax. Tomorrow my father and I are leaving to visit my mother's sister in the French Savoie. We'll be attending another wedding and taking a vacation at the same time."

"That's right. Your father usually goes away this time of year."

He nodded. "I'm not sure how soon we'll be back, but I promise I'll be here for your June appointment with the doctor."

June... He'd be gone several weeks at least. She fought to keep her expression from showing her devastating disappointment.

The limo drove up to his private entrance to the palace. "I'll come to your apartment in a half hour, unless you need more time."

"Knowing that you have a healthy appetite, thirty minutes is probably all you should have to wait for dinner."

The flash of a satisfied white smile was the last thing she saw before he exited the limo.

It stayed with her all the way to her suite. Her hands trembled as she removed her hat and put it on the closet shelf. Next came the dress and her shoes.

After Abby had put on jeans with an elastic waist band and a pink short-sleeved top, she redid her hair. While she fastened it with a tortoiseshell clip, she was assailed by the memory of Vincenzo's eyes as she'd climbed in the limo. They'd been alive and there was a throbbing moment when…

No. She was mistaken. The prince was a man, after all, and couldn't have helped looking while she was at a disadvantage. Furious with herself for ascribing more to the moment than was there, she lifted the phone to ring Angelina for her dinner tray, then thought the better of it. Vincenzo had made it clear he was orchestrating the rest of this evening.

If she wasn't careful, she could get used to this kind of attention. But once she'd had the baby, her association with the prince would be over. By November he could easily be involved with another woman, who had the right credentials for another marriage.

Her thoughts darted ahead to his trip with the king. Since Vincenzo had recently returned from a trip that had lasted weeks, she doubted he'd be accompanying his father because he needed another vacation.

In all probability there was someone the king and his aunt wanted him to meet. With a baby on the way, he needed a suitable wife who was already situated at the palace to take over the duties of a mother the minute Abby delivered. But the thought of another woman being a mother to Abby's baby killed her.

This baby was Abby's baby. She couldn't possibly separate herself from it now. She'd been imagining the day she held it in her arms, the clothes she'd buy, the nursery she'd create. No other woman would love this baby as fiercely as the way Abby already did.

But Vincenzo was the father and he'd been born to fulfill his duties. One of them at the moment was to make certain Abby felt secure while she was pregnant with the next royal heir of Arancia. She knew better than to read any-thing more into what was going on. He was doing his best while trying to cope with the pain of his loss. There was only one way for her to handle this and keep her sanity at the same time.

He needs a friend, Abby. Be one to him.

A half hour later Vincenzo arrived at her apartment. He'd changed out of his suit into chinos and a polo shirt. He looked so fabulous, she tried not stare at him. He'd tucked a DVD under his arm. She flashed him her friendliest smile. "You're right on time."

"In the business I'm in, you have to be."

A quiet laugh escaped her lips. "Well, tonight you can forget business for once. Come right in and make yourself at home."

"If it's all right with you, I'll put this in the machine."

She closed the door after him and folded her arms. "Aren't you going to show me the cover?"

"I'd rather surprise you." In a minute he'd in-serted it so they could watch it on the living room couch when they were ready.

"All I have to offer you is soda from the fridge in the kitchen."

"I'll drink what you're drinking."

"It's boring lemonade."

"Sounds good."

She didn't call him a liar again. He was probably used to some kind of alcohol at the end of the day, but was going out of his way to make her comfortable. This man was spoiling her rotten.

"Excuse me while I get it." When she came out of the kitchen, she found him on her terrace leaning against the balustrade. "In the States we say 'a penny for them.'" She handed him a can.

He straightened and took it from her. "I'll give you one guess." He popped the lid and drank the contents in one go. Abby was thirsty, too, and followed suit, but could only drink half of hers before needing a breath.

"A name for your baby."

"It has already been picked, whether it's a boy or a girl. Actually, I was thinking about your plans after the baby's born," he said on a more serious note.

So had she… Since that terrible morning with the queen, she'd decided that living anywhere in Arancia wouldn't be a good idea after all. "You're giving me a complex, you know."

A frown marred his handsome features. "In what way?"

"You worry too much about everything, so maybe what I tell you will help. The other night my father came over and we had a long talk. Before Christmas, in fact, before I even knew you were looking for a surrogate, Dad was planning to resign his position here and move back to the States. He says his assistant, Ernesto, is more than ready to take over."

Stillness enveloped Vincenzo for an overly long moment. "Does my father know about this?"

"Not yet. He plans to tell him soon. We have extended family in Rhode Island, where I was born."

"But your father has family here in Arancia, too."

"That's true, but he's been offered a position at a private firm there I know he will enjoy. He won't leave until after I have the baby. Though I had thoughts of living in Arancia and working at the firm with Carolena, I can't abide the idea of him being so far away. Therefore I'll be moving back with him and plan to study for the Rhode Island and New York bar exams. So you see? That's one worry you can cross off your long list."

During the quiet that followed, she heard a knock on the door. He moved before she did to answer it. Angelina had arrived with their dinner. Vincenzo thanked her and pushed the cart to the terrace, where they could sit to enjoy their meal while they looked out over the view.

Once they started eating, he focused his attention on her. "Are you close with family there?"

"We've all kept in touch. Mom took me for visits several times a year."

"I remember. The grounds seemed emptier then."

Abby wished he hadn't said that. Though it was nice to see family, she lived to get back to Vincenzo.

"After she died, Dad always sent me to stay

with my mother's sister and her husband at Easter. I have a couple of fun cousins close to my age. It will be wonderful to live around all of them again. My aunt's a lot like my mom, so nice and kindhearted."

That part was the truth, as far as it went. These years in Arancia were a dream that had to end, but she wouldn't allow herself to think about leaving the country, about leaving *him*. Not yet.

"If you've finished," he said all of a sudden, "shall we go inside and start the movie?"

"Marvelous idea. I can't wait to see what you picked out. Something American and silly, I presume, like *Back to the Beach*."

A mysterious smile appeared to chase away his earlier somber look. She got up from the chair before he could help her and walked in the living room to turn it on.

CHAPTER SIX

ABBY'S REVELATION HAD put Vincenzo off the last of his dinner. He'd meant it when he'd told her he missed her presence during her vacations out of the country. Because of their situation, Abby had always been natural with him and treated him like a friend. No artifice. Though he'd been six years older, she'd been there in the background of his life for years. But when she went away next time, she wouldn't be returning.

The sense of loss was already hitting him. He was staggered by the depth of his feelings. When she'd opened the door to him awhile ago, he'd discovered her in yet another new maternity outfit. This time she wore flattering casual attire. Yet no matter how she played down her assets, nothing could disguise the fact that she was a very desirable woman.

Now that she was carrying his child, how

could he not notice her or stop certain thoughts from creeping into his mind without his volition? Abby had become as precious to him as the little life growing inside of her.

Earlier, once he'd entered the church and scanned the guests, he'd spotted the hat and the face beneath it. For the rest of the ceremony he couldn't take his eyes off her. She'd lit up the interior like an exotic orchid among the greenery.

"My Little Chickadee?" The excitement in her voice was all he could have hoped for. She swung around to face him with a brilliant smile. "Trust you to manage getting hold of a copy of it. This was Mom's favorite Mae West film. W.C. Fields is in it, too. This movie is hilarious."

"While you stretch out on the couch and put your legs up, I'll sit in the chair with the ottoman."

"Vincenzo—I didn't literally mean I needed to do that. My feet aren't swollen yet!"

He took his place in the chair anyway. "From what I saw as you got in the limo, I couldn't detect any problem in that department, either, but as you reminded me a week ago, I'm only a man and don't have a clue about a woman."

While the film got underway, she curled up on the end of the couch. He saw her shoulders shaking with silent laughter. "You'll never let me live that down. Apparently you have a photographic memory. I bet Gianna could tell me what a maddening brother you were at times."

He grinned at her. "It's a good thing she's not here to reveal my secrets."

Abby flicked him a narrowed gaze. "Oh, I heard a few."

"Like what, for instance?"

"Like the time you and your friends brought some girls to the palace and sneaked them into the pool at three in the morning to go skinny-dipping. I know it's true because I heard about it from my father later. He'd been awakened in the middle of the night by some of the security men."

He spread his hands. "What can I say? My life has been an open book in more ways than one. Were you scandalized?"

"I was only fifteen at the time and wondered how any girl could be so daring."

"But not the guys?"

"No. It's in your nature, which has been written into your Roman mythology. Wasn't it the goddess Diana, Jupiter's favorite daughter, to whom he swore he wouldn't make her marry and allowed her to hunt by the light of the moon? She loved skinny-dipping, and naturally all the young men came to watch."

The laughter rolled out of Vincenzo. He couldn't help it.

Abby kept a straight face. "But sadly for them, when she caught them, she turned them into stags. Of course, that was centuries ago. Today it's the other way around. The teenaged girls are scandalized by prudes like me."

When he could find his voice, he said, "You mean I couldn't have talked you into it?"

"Not on your life!"

She could always make him laugh, and the film *was* hilarious. He'd been waiting for the famous line she'd impersonated. When it came, he realized Abby had sounded just like the legendary actress.

After the film ended, she got up and turned off the machine. "I wish I'd had an older brother. You and Gianna were lucky to grow up together. One day when you marry again, hopefully you'll be able to have another baby so your first one won't grow up to be an only child."

The thought of taking another wife sent a chill through him. He knew when his father had insisted Vincenzo accompany him on this next trip it had been motivated by an agenda that had little to do with the need for a vacation.

"Were you ever lonely, Abby?"

"Not in the sense you mean, because being the brightest light on my parents' horizon was my only reality. I knew nothing else. But when I think of you and Gianna, especially the two of you growing up in a royal household, I can see how great that would have been for you. She told me she went to bat for you when you got into trouble with your father. There's nothing like the power of sibling love."

With pure grace she curled her leg underneath

her again and sat down. "Did you ever have to help her out of a spot?"

"Many times. She wanted money. When I didn't feel like carrying out some official function, I'd bribe her to do it for me."

Abby laughed. "At what cost?"

"Pocket money. Our parents kept us both on a strict allowance."

"Good for them! I always liked them, but that admission puts them on an even higher level in—"

Vincenzo's cell phone rang, breaking in on her. "Sorry." He pulled it out of his pocket and checked the caller ID. "Excuse me for a moment, Abby. I have to take this."

"Of course."

He moved to the terrace, out of earshot. *"Pronto?"*

"I'm sorry to disturb you, but the queen was insistent you call her back immediately."

"Do you have any idea why, Marcello?"

"No, except that she'd been talking to the king first."

He had an idea what this might be about.

Something told him he needed to put out another fire, but first he needed to talk to his father. "I'll take care of it. *Grazie.*"

When he walked back inside, Abby was waiting for him near the front door. "Duty calls, right?" She'd given him no choice but to leave. "Thank you for this lovely and unexpected evening."

"I enjoyed it, too. Keep the DVD as a reminder of your mother," he said when she was about to hand it him.

"You're too generous, but I'll treasure it."

"That's the idea," he murmured.

She put a hand to her throat. "As soon as you came in from the terrace, I could tell by your face something was wrong. I hope it's nothing too serious."

If his hunch was right, then it *was* serious. But for once, this had nothing to do with Abby. He could thank the Roman gods for that, at least.

Too bad he couldn't get rid of a certain dangerous vision in his mind of joining Abby the Huntress in that forest pool and making love to her before her father discovered them and *he* turned Vincenzo into a stag.

He ground his teeth absently. "So do I, Abby. I'll see you at the clinic for your next appointment. Though I know you'll follow the doctor's orders, I have to say this anyway. Take meticulous care of yourself." June sounded an eternity away.

Her eyes had gone a smoky blue. "You, too, Your Highness. Your baby's going to need you."

Vincenzo turned from her before he couldn't and took off for the other region of the palace at a fast clip.

When he reached his apartment, he decided it wouldn't do any good to call his father first. Without hesitation he phoned Michelina's mother to get this over with.

"Thank you for returning my call, Vincenzo."

"Of course. How are you getting along, Bianca?"

"How do you think? My world has fallen apart. I didn't believe it could get worse until I talked with your father. He informed me you're going on vacation tomorrow to stay with the *duc de Chambery.* If you hadn't chosen Michelina, you would have married his granddaughter Odile, who's still single. That would be a humiliation for our family if you choose her now. I'm telling you I won't—"

"Bianca?" he broke in on her. He had it in his heart to feel sorry for this woman who was grieving over her daughter. "You don't need to say another word. I know exactly how Michelina felt about her. I never considered marriage to Odile and I'll make you a solemn vow now that I never will. Does that answer your question?"

Her weeping finally stopped and all he heard was sniffing. "But you'll take another bride."

He'd braced his back against the door to his den and closed his eyes. "To be frank with you, I don't plan on marrying again. When Father is no longer alive, I may step down so Gianna can take over the business of ruling Arancia. My first duty is going to be to Michelina's and my child."

Her gasp came over the phone loud and clear. "I don't believe you."

"Which part?" he bit out.

"You don't fool me. We both know the only reason why you'd give up the throne…"

Her insinuation was perfectly clear. She'd all but accused Abby of going after Vincenzo. He'd been waiting for her to start in on him. This was just the first volley.

He heard the click, severing their connection.

"Congratulations, Signorina Loretto. You show no problems so far. It means you've been following directions to the letter." Abby could thank Vincenzo for that. "How is the nausea?"

"I hardly ever notice it anymore."

"Good. Your measurements are fine. Be sure to keep your feet up for a little each day after work."

"I will. How big is the baby by now?"

"Um, three inches. You're growing."

"I know. I already prefer lying on my side."

The doctor smiled. "I'll let the prince know that at your sixteen-weeks' checkup we'll do an ultrasound, which should reveal the gender of that special baby."

Abby didn't know if Vincenzo wanted to be surprised and wait until after the baby was delivered, or if he was anxious to know right away. But it was his business, not hers.

"You can get dressed now and I'll see you in another month. Be sure you keep coming in on a weekly basis for your blood pressure check. I'll give Vincenzo the full report when he's back. He'll be delighted. As for Dr. Greco, he said for you to call him when the two of you can come in."

"Thank you, Doctor."

Abby put on her white sundress with the brown-trimmed white bolero top and left for the office. Her father had told her the king had returned to the palace three days ago. That meant Vincenzo was still in France.

With a woman who might possibly take Michelina's place one day?

Abby was used to him honoring every commitment to her. The fact that he hadn't come today shouldn't have mattered, but it did. She missed him and would be lying if she didn't admit that to herself.

The show-cause hearing at the court yesterday had persuaded the judge to hear the Giordano case in August. Abby was thrilled with the outcome and knew his decision had frustrated Signor Masala's attorney. She wanted to share the good news with Vincenzo and thank him, but it would have to wait.

She was starting to get a taste of what it would be like when he wasn't in her life anymore. Not liking that he'd become the focal point of her thoughts, she phoned her father after she got in the limo and invited him to a home-cooked dinner at her apartment that evening. She planned to fry chicken and make scones, the kind her mom always made. He loved them. But to her disappointment, he couldn't come until the following night.

Once she got to work, she invited Carolena to the palace to have dinner with her at the pool. Abby would lend her one of the bikinis she hadn't worn yet. Thankfully her friend was thrilled to be invited and they rode home together in the limo at the end of the day.

"Am I in heaven or what?"

They'd finished eating and had spent time in the pool. Now they were treading water. Abby laughed at her friend. "I've been asking myself that same question since we moved here years ago." She was tempted to tell Carolena her future plans, but thought the better of it until closer to the delivery date. "I think I'll do one more lap and then I'll be done for the night."

She pushed off, doing the backstroke. When she reached the other side and turned to hold on to the side, she saw blood and let out a small cry.

"What's wrong?" Carolena swam over to her. "Oh—you've got a nosebleed."

"I don't know why." She pinched her nose with her thumb and index finger.

"I'll get a towel."

Abby followed her to the steps and got out.

"Sit on the chair." She handed Abby her beach towel.

After a minute she said, "It's not stopping."

"Keep holding while I call your doctor. Is his number programmed in your cell phone?"

"Yes. Press three."

Angelina came out on the patio to clear the table, but let out an alarmed sound the second she saw the blood on the towel and hurried away.

By now Carolena was off the phone. "The doctor wants you to lean forward on the chair and keep pressing your nostrils together for ten or fifteen minutes. Breathe through your mouth. It should stop. Apparently pregnant women get nosebleeds, so not to worry. If it doesn't stop soon, we'll call him back."

"Okay." Before another minute passed, Vincenzo came running toward her. He was back!

"Abby—" Without hesitation he hunkered down next to her. The fear in his eyes was a revelation to her.

"I'm all right, Vincenzo. My nose started to bleed, but I think it has stopped now."

He reached for his cell phone. "I'm calling Dr. DeLuca."

"Carolena already contacted him for me. I'm fine, honestly!"

She removed the towel to show him the episode was over. Already she felt like a fraud.

"Don't move." He got up to get her beach robe and put it around her shoulders. His touch sent fingers of delight through her body. "It's cooler out here now."

"Thank you. I don't believe you've been introduced to my friend, Carolena Baretti. Carolena, this is His Royal Highness Prince Vincenzo."

"Thank heaven you were here for her, Signorina Baretti. I'm very pleased to meet you."

"The pleasure is mine, Your Highness. Dr. De-Luca said the increased blood flow with pregnancy sometimes produces nosebleeds. She's supposed to stay put for a few minutes so she won't get light-headed when she stands. He'll be relieved to know the bleeding has stopped."

"I'll call him and tell him right now."

While Vincenzo walked out of earshot to make the phone call, Carolena moved closer to Abby. Her brows lifted as she stared at her. "When he saw you holding that towel to your face, I thought he was going to have a heart attack."

"I know he was afraid something had happened to the baby."

Carolena shook her head. "From the look in his eyes, it wasn't the baby he was worried about," she whispered. "If a man ever looked at me like that…"

Abby's heart thudded against her ribs. "You're imagining things." But inwardly she was shaken by the look in his eyes. It was that same look he'd given her after she'd recovered on the boat that black day, as if she'd meant the world to him.

What a time for him to return from his trip! She looked an utter mess.

Vincenzo walked toward her. "If you feel all right, I'll help you get back to your apartment."

"I'm fine. Carolena will help me."

"We'll both help." The authority in his voice silenced her.

Together the three of them left the pool. Carolena brought all their things while Vincenzo stayed at Abby's side. When they reached her suite, her friend changed her clothes and announced she was leaving.

"I'll have a limousine waiting for you at the

entrance, *Signorina*. Again, my thanks for your help."

"Abby's the best."

"So are you." Abby hugged her friend.

"Thanks for dinner. See you at work tomorrow."

The minute the door closed, Abby glanced at Vincenzo. "If you'll excuse me, I'll take a quick shower."

"Don't hurry on my account. I'm not going anywhere."

That fluttery sensation in her stomach had taken over again. It happened whenever he came near. She rushed into the bathroom and got busy making herself presentable once more. After drying her hair with a clean towel, she brushed it the best she could and put on a clean blouse and skirt.

The nosebleed had definitely stopped. Just one of the surprises brought on by the pregnancy. She couldn't complain. So far she'd been very lucky.

Again she found him out on the terrace, which was her favorite place, too, especially at night.

He looked sensational in anything he wore. Tonight it was a silky blue shirt and khakis. "Did the doctor reassure you?"

He turned and put his hands on his hips, the ultimate male. "To a point. I'm much more relieved now that I see you walking around without further problem."

"Don't do it," she warned him.

Those black brows furrowed. "Do what?"

"Start feeling guilty again because I'm in this situation."

"If you want to know the stark, staring truth, guilt is the last thing on my mind. I'm worrying about the next time you get another one. What if Carolena hadn't been with you?"

"I had the usual nosebleed here and there growing up. They've always stopped on their own, as this one did tonight, even though she was with me. But if I'd been alone and needed help, I would have called out for Angelina. Don't forget that at work I'm never alone."

Her logic finally sank in and his frown disappeared. "I'm sorry I didn't make it back in time for our appointment with Dr. Greco. If I hadn't been detained, I would have been in the pool with you when this happened."

A thrill of forbidden excitement shot through her body to hear that.

"Everything's fine. We'll reschedule when it's convenient for you."

His dark gaze wandered over her. "Dr. De-Luca says you're in excellent health."

"You see?" She smiled.

"He's going to do an ultrasound on you next month."

"Is the helicopter daddy anxious to know if he's going to have a boy or a girl?"

"I'm not sure yet. For the moment all I care about is that you and the baby stay healthy."

"That's my prime concern, too. But maybe by then you'll have made up your mind and want to know if the kingdom can expect a prince or a princess."

"Maybe. Let's go back inside where it's warmer so you'll stay well."

When Abby had told her father that Vincenzo was a worrywart, he'd laughed his head off. If he could see them now…

She did his bidding and walked through to the kitchen, where she opened the fridge. He followed her. "Orange juice all right?" she asked.

"Sounds good."

Abby chuckled. "No, it doesn't. Why don't you have some wine from the cupboard? You look like it might do you some good."

"Soda is fine."

"A warrior to the end. That's you." She pulled out two cans and took them over to the table, where he helped her before sitting down. They popped their lids at the same time. The noise was so loud they both let out a laugh, the first she'd heard come from him tonight. A smiling Vincenzo was a glorious sight. "How was your trip?"

"Which one are you talking about?"

She almost choked on her drink. "You took two trips?"

He nodded. "I only flew in an hour ago from Gemelli."

Abby blinked. "I didn't realize you were going there."

"It wasn't on the schedule, but Bianca slipped on a stair in the palace and broke her hip."

"Oh, no—"

"Valentino phoned me after it happened. It was the day Father and I were scheduled to come home. We agreed I should fly to Gemelli to be with her."

Whatever Abby had been thinking about the reason for his absence, she'd been wrong and promised herself to stop speculating about anything to do with him from now on.

"Is she in terrible pain?"

"At first, but she's going to be fine with therapy. We had several long talks. If there can be any good in her getting hurt, it seems to have softened her somewhat in her attitude about the coming event. Despite her misgivings, the idea of a grandchild has taken hold."

"That's wonderful, Vincenzo."

"She's missing Michelina."

"Of course." Abby took another long drink. "You must be so relieved to be on better terms with her."

He stared at her through veiled eyes. "I am. But when Angelina told me about you—"

"You thought you were facing another crisis," she finished for him. "Well, as you can see, all is well. Did your father have a good vacation?"

Vincenzo finished off his soda before answering her. "No."

"I'm sorry to hear that."

"He brought his troubles on himself."

"Is he ill?"

"If only it were that simple."

"Vincenzo—" She didn't know whether to laugh or cry. "What a thing to say."

"Before I was betrothed, my parents arranged for me to meet the princesses on their short list of candidates, carefully chosen by the extended family."

Abby lowered her head.

"It came down to two, Michelina Cavelli and Odile Levallier, the granddaughter of the *duc de Chambery.* Both were nice-looking at their age, but of the two, I preferred Michelina, who wasn't as headstrong or spoiled."

"I can't imagine being in your situation."

"When you're born into a royal family, it's just the way it is. You don't know anything else. If I'd had a different personality, perhaps I would have rebelled and run away. I was still a royal teenager at the time and knew I had years before I needed to think about getting married, so I didn't let it bother me too much."

Her head came up and she eyed him soberly. "Were you ever in love?"

"At least four times that I recall."

"You're serious."

"Deadly so. In fact it might have been seven or eight times."

Seven or eight?

"Those poor women who'd loved you, knowing they didn't stand a chance of becoming your wife. Did you spend time with Michelina over the years, too?"

"Some. When my father decided it was time for me to marry, I saw her more often. She had always been good-looking and smart. We enjoyed riding horses and playing tennis. She was a great athlete, and loved the water. I could see myself married to her."

"When did you actually fall in love with her?"

He cocked his head. "Would it shock you if I told you never?"

Never?

Shaken to the core, Abby got up from the table and put their cans in the wastebasket.

"I can see that I have."

She whirled around. "But she loved you so much—"

Quiet surrounded them before he nodded. "Now you're disillusioned."

Abby leaned against the counter so she wouldn't fall down. "The loving way you treated her, no one would ever have guessed."

He got up from the table and walked over to her. "Except Michelina, her mother, my parents and now you… We both wanted a baby to make our marriage work."

She couldn't believe it had never worked, not in the sense he meant. Talk about a shocking revelation.…

So *that* was the real reason they'd gone so far as to find a surrogate and flaunt convention. It explained Michelina's desperation and her decision not to tell the queen until it was too late to stop it. No wonder Bianca feared another woman coming into Vincenzo's life. The pieces of the puzzle were starting to come together. She could hardly breathe.

"Obviously we were willing to do anything. Again we were presented with a short list. This time it had the names and histories of the women available and suitable to carry our child."

She lifted pleading eyes to him. "Will you tell me the truth about something, Vincenzo?" Her voice throbbed. "Did Michelina want me?"

"Of course. She'd always liked you. She said you had a wonderful sense of humor and found you charming. When she learned you were on that list of possible surrogates who'd passed all the physical tests, like me she was surprised, but happy, too. Our choice was unanimous."

Unable to be this close to him, she left the kitchen for the living room and sat down on the end of the couch. He again chose the chair with the ottoman. They were like an old married couple sitting around before they went to bed.

Abby wished that particular thought hadn't

entered her mind. With Vincenzo's revelation, the world as she'd known it had changed, and nothing would ever be the same again. All these years and he hadn't been in love with his wife? He'd been in love seven or eight times, but they didn't count because they weren't royal. She needed to move the conversation onto another subject.

"You were telling me about your father."

Vincenzo let out a sigh. "He wants me to marry again before the baby is born." He came out with it bluntly, rocking her world once more.

"In the beginning Odile was his first choice, only because of his close association with the *duc*. It would be advantageous to both our countries. She hasn't married yet and he feels she would make a fine mother. If she's there from the moment the baby is born, then she'll bond with it."

Abby sucked in her breath. "Does Odile still care for you?" It was a stupid question. The fact that she was still single was glaring proof, but she'd had to say it.

"She thinks she does, but that's because no

one else has come along yet whom her grand-father finds suitable. I told Father I couldn't possibly marry Odile because I don't have the slightest feeling for her."

Unable to stand it, she jumped up from the couch. "This is like a chess game, moving kings and queens around without any regard for human feeling!"

One black brow lifted. "That's where you're wrong. My mother-in-law certainly has a lot of feelings on the subject."

"She knows why you went to France?"

He sat forward. "Every royal household has its spies. That's why she phoned me before I left to tell me she wouldn't stand for it if I ended up marrying Odile. Michelina had been frightened I'd choose Odile over her in the first place."

Incredible. "What did you tell the queen?"

"That there was no chance of it because I don't plan to marry again. For once I'm going to do what my heart dictates and be a good fa-ther to my child, period."

Abby started trembling. "I'm sure she didn't believe you." Abby didn't believe it either. He was too young to live out the rest of his life alone. But if he had to marry another royal he didn't love…

"No, but it doesn't matter, because I've made my decision."

"Don't you have to be married to be king?"

"That has been the tradition over the centuries, but Father's still very much alive. If the time comes when someone else must rule, my sister will do it. So in answer to your question, *that's* how my father's trip went. Why don't we get onto another subject and talk about your court case? How did it go?"

She sat back down, still trying to get her head around everything he'd told her. "You know very well how it went. The judge had it put on his calendar for mid-August."

"Excellent. That relieves some of your stress, which can only be good for the baby. What other cases are you dealing with?"

"I don't know. I—I can't think right now," Abby stammered. She honestly couldn't.

"Let's watch a little television. There's usually a movie on this time of night." He got up from the chair and reached for the remote on the coffee table.

"You don't need to stay with me, Vincenzo. The doctor assured you I'm all right. I know you must be exhausted after being in Gemelli. Please go."

A fierce look marred his features. "You want me to?"

A small gasp escaped. She'd offended him again. "Of course not. It's just that I don't want you to feel you have to babysit me."

"There's nothing I'd rather do. Everything I care about is in this room, and I've been away for weeks."

Shaken again by his honesty, Abby felt his frustration and understood it before he turned on the TV and sat back down again. One glance and she saw that the prince was a channel grazer. Nothing seemed to suit him. On impulse she got up from the couch.

"I'll be right back. I've got something for you." She made a stop at the bathroom, a frequent habit these days. Then she went to the bedroom and pulled her thick scrapbook out of the bottom dresser drawer. She'd had the leather cover engraved in gold letters: *The Prince of Arancia.* She hoped this might brighten his mood.

"Here." She walked over to him. "I'll trade you this for the remote."

He eyed her in surprise. When he got a look at the cover, he let out an exclamation. "I thought this was going to be a gift for the christening."

"I've changed my mind." Abby had compassion for him and his father, who wanted his son to be happily married and was trying to make it happen in the only way he could think of as king. "You need to see what an impact you've made on the life of your subjects."

Maybe this album would make Vincenzo realize what an important man he was. To live out his life alone wasn't natural or healthy.

"I know the court has a historian who records everything, but this is more personal, with some of my own photos and articles I've found interesting from various magazines and newspapers coming from the U.S. Dad's been receiving the Stateside news for years and I read everything right along with him."

From the moment Vincenzo opened the cover, he went away from her mentally. While she watched the news, he turned page after page, thoughtfully perusing each one. No sound came out of him for at least an hour.

Eventually he closed it and looked over at her. "For the first time in my life, I know what it feels like to have your life flash before your eyes. I don't know what to say, Abby. I'm speechless."

"You're probably tired from viewing all the good works you've done over the years. I hope you realize you've *never* received negative press. Do you have any idea what a great accomplishment that is?"

He studied her as if he'd never seen her before. "I hope *you* realize I've never received a gift like this. You've touched me beyond my ability to express," he said in a husky voice she felt all the way to her toes.

"I'm glad if you're pleased. I consider it an honor to be a friend of yours, and an even greater honor to be the person you and Michelina chose to carry your child. Only a few more months before he or she is here."

She had the impression he wasn't listening to her. "All these photos of yours. I wasn't aware you'd taken them."

"While I was darting around on the grounds with my little camera, I took a lot of pictures and sometimes you were there."

"You got me on my motorcycle!"

"If you have a boy, he'll be thrilled to find out you didn't always behave with perfect decorum. I daresay he'll love it that you were a daredevil. The skinny-dipping I missed, because I had to be in bed and asleep by eleven."

Low laughter rumbled out of him. "I can be thankful your father was the head of security and made sure his daughter minded him."

She smiled. "Do you think you'll be a strict father if you have a girl?"

He got up from the chair and put the album on the coffee table before staring at her. "Probably."

"But since kindness is part of your nature, she won't mind."

He rubbed the back of his neck, looking tired. "Have you had any feelings yet whether you might be having a boy or a girl, Abby? I understand some women instinctively know."

"I've heard that, too, but since I'm not the mother, that's not going to happen to me." Secretly she didn't want him to know how involved she really was with this baby and that she thought about it all the time. "However, there's no law that says the father can't feel inspiration about his own unborn child."

He shook his head. "No indication yet."

"Well, you've got a month before there's the possibility of your finding out. That is, if you want to."

"If it's a girl, Michelina wanted to name her Julietta after her grandmother on her mother's side."

"That's beautiful. And if it's a boy?"

Their gazes held for a moment. "Maximilliano, after three kings in the Di Laurentis line. I'll call him Max."

"I love that name!" she cried. "We had a wonderful Irish setter named Max. He died before we moved here."

Vincenzo looked surprised. "I didn't know

that. Why didn't your father get another one when you settled in your apartment?"

"The loss was so great, neither he nor Mom could think about getting another one. They kept saying maybe one day, but that moment never came. Did your family have a pet?"

He nodded. "Several, but by my later teens I was gone so much, my mother was the one who took care of them and they worshipped her."

"That's sweet."

"Whether I have a boy or a girl, I'll make certain they grow up with a dog. It's important."

"I couldn't agree more. Whether you've had a good or bad day, they're always there for you and so loving. My cousin and I liked little creatures. I once kept a cockatoo, a turtle, a snake and a hamster. When each of them died—not all at the same time, of course," she said with a laugh, "Max helped me get through their funerals. Daddy used to say the best psychiatrist is a puppy licking your face."

"Abby..." There was a world of warmth when he said her name. "No wonder Piero's father called you the little nurse."

"It's a good thing he didn't get together with my father to compare notes. If you got him alone, Daddy would tell you I probably killed them all off without meaning to."

She loved the sound of his laughter so much, Abby never wanted it to stop. But for the sake of her sanity and her heart, it was imperative he leave. Quickly she got up from the couch and handed him the scrapbook.

"This is yours to keep. You once saved my life, and now you're taking such good care of me, my thanks will never be enough. Now it's time someone took care of you. Please don't be mad at me if I tell you to go to bed. You look exhausted." She walked to the door and opened it. If he didn't leave, she was on the verge of begging him to stay the night.

"Good night, Your Highness."

In the weeks that followed, Vincenzo made certain his schedule was packed so tight with work he wouldn't be tempted to spend every free moment at Abby's apartment. Though he phoned her every morning before she went to work to know how she felt, he stayed away from her.

The night she'd given him the album, she'd shown him the door before he was ready to leave. When he'd told her the true situation that had existed between him and Michelina, there'd been a definite shift in the universe. He didn't regret his decision to tell her. At this point in the pregnancy, they shared an intimacy that demanded she understand what his marriage had been like so there'd be honesty between them.

The day of the ultrasound was here. His greatest concern was the health of the baby. If something was wrong, then he'd deal with it. Vincenzo had gone back and forth in his mind on the subject of gender and finally decided he didn't want to know. That way both sides of his family would have to go on speculating until the delivery. As for himself, he preferred to be surprised.

He had the limousine pulled around to his private entrance. When Abby appeared in a kelly-green dress with flowing sleeves and a high waist, he lost his breath for a moment. She was finally looking pregnant and more beautiful than she knew with her silvery-gold hair upswept and caught with a comb.

Dr. DeLuca met them in his office first and smiled. "This is the big day. Are you ready for it?"

"It's very exciting," Abby answered. Though she seemed calm, Vincenzo knew she had to be nervous.

"Will you come in to watch the ultrasound, Vincenzo?"

"Yes!"

Abby looked stunned. "You really want to?"

Vincenzo caught her blue gaze. "I've been waiting for this from the moment we found out you were pregnant."

"I—I'm excited, too," she stammered, rather breathlessly, he thought.

"Excellent," the doctor said. "If you'll come this way with me. It won't take long."

They followed him through another door to the ultrasound room. The doctor told Vincenzo to sit at the side of the bed while Abby lay down. His heart picked up speed to realize this moment had come. He didn't intend to miss a second of this whole process.

Abby's face had blushed when he'd said yes. He knew she'd been trying her hardest to keep her professional distance, but at this point in the pregnancy that was impossible. Having a baby was an intimate experience and she'd never been "just a surrogate" to him.

Over the last few months she'd come to be his whole world. It was miraculous that a sonogram could see inside her gorgeous body, where his baby was growing. The body he'd once rescued from the sea. How could he have known that one day she'd carry his child? He couldn't think about anything else.

Michelina was the mother of his child, but right now his focus was on Abby while the doctor put special gel on her stomach. For several nights he'd had trouble sleeping while his mind thought of all the things that might be wrong with the baby.

She shared a searching glance with Vincenzo as the doctor moved the transducer around her belly. Suddenly they both heard a heartbeat coming from the monitor. The doctor pointed to the screen. "There's your baby. The heart sounds perfect."

"Oh, Vincenzo—our baby! There it is!" In the moment of truth, her guard had come down, thrilling him with her honesty. As for himself, he couldn't believe what he was seeing and reached for her hand. She squeezed it hard. "It looks like it's praying."

The doctor nodded with a smile. "Nice size, coming along beautifully. No abnormalities I can see. So far everything looks good. This test can't detect all birth defects, but it's a wonderful diagnostic tool and tells me the pregnancy and your baby are both on the right track."

Relief poured off Vincenzo in waves. He looked into her tear-filled eyes. Without conscious thought he leaned over and kissed her mouth. "You're a wonder, Abby," he whispered. "You're giving me the world."

"I'm so thankful everything's all right."

The doctor cleared his throat. "Do you two want to know the gender?"

"That's up to Vincenzo," she said first.

He'd already made up his mind. "I'd rather wait and be surprised."

"Very well. Here are some pictures for you to keep." The doctor explained what Vincenzo was seeing, but he didn't have to, because the shape of the baby was self-evident and filled him with awe. If Michelina were here, the tears would be overflowing. "The fetus is four and half inches long and developing well."

Vincenzo put them in his jacket pocket. "Doctor? How's Abby?"

He removed his glasses. "As you can see, she's fine. No more nosebleeds?" She shook her head. "I'd say Abby is in perfect health. If she continues to do what I told her and rest a little more often after her swims, she should get through this pregnancy in great shape."

That was all Vincenzo wanted to hear, though it didn't take away his guilt that she was risking her life to give him this baby. "Thank you, Dr. DeLuca."

After the older man left the room, Abby got

up off the table to fix her dress. "Can you believe it? Our baby's fine."

"I'm glad to hear you say *our* baby. It is our baby now, Abby. And I'm overjoyed to know you're fine, too." He got up from the chair. "This calls for a major celebration." As they walked out of the hospital to the waiting limo, he said, "After work, we're leaving for a weekend aboard the yacht. The doctor wants you to rest and swim and do whatever you like. I'll let you decide our destination once we leave port."

She looked startled. "How can you get away?"

"Very easily."

Once inside the limo, she turned to him. "Vincenzo? Do you think this would be wise?"

A dark frown broke out on his face, erasing his earlier happiness. "Obviously you don't."

"When I tell my father where we're going, he'll tell me it's not a good idea. Already he's talking about our move back to the States. I can tell he's getting nervous about you and me spending any more time together that isn't absolutely necessary."

Vincenzo's jaw hardened. "Has he spoken to my father yet about leaving?"

"Yes. Last night."

That was news to Vincenzo. "How did he take it?"

"He wanted to know the reasons and asked him about our extended family back home."

"Was my father upset?"

"No. He said he'd been expecting it for some time."

Vincenzo grimaced. "Then he didn't try to dissuade your father from leaving."

"No, and we both know why." Her voice trembled. "You and I have shared a unique relationship for many years. The baby's on the way and Michelina is gone. Guilio wants you to take a wife ASAP."

Vincenzo's dark head reared. "Father knows my feelings on the subject. I'm not planning to get married again and am already looking into finding a full-time nanny to help me with the baby."

"You're serious—"

His mouth tightened. "Do you think I would

make that up? If so, then you don't know me at all."

"I don't think Guilio has any idea you mean it. The situation is even worse than I'd feared," she muttered.

"What situation?"

"You know exactly what I'm talking about. The only reason I felt all right about becoming a surrogate was because you and Michelina were a team. But she's not here anymore and *I* am."

He sat forward. "I still don't understand you."

"Yes, you do, even if you won't admit it."

"Admit what?"

"You and I have shared a unique relationship over the years. With Michelina gone and me carrying your child, our friendship is now suspect. The fact that your father isn't begging Dad to stay on tells me it will please him once we've left Arancia for good. He wants you to take Odile on the yacht, not me."

"You haven't been listening to me," he ground out.

Her heart thudded harder, because she could feel how upset he'd become. "Vincenzo, you're in a very rocky place right now and grabbing at what is easy and familiar because I've always been around. But you're not thinking straight. For us to go on the yacht could spell disaster. That's why I'm not going with you."

He said nothing while her guilt was warring with her heart, but her guilt won. "Your wife has only been gone a few months. Of course you haven't been able to figure out your future yet. You're in a state of limbo and will be until the baby is born."

"Have you finished?" came his icy question.

"Not quite yet." As long as she'd been this brave, she needed to get it all said. When she felt her lips, they still tingled from Vincenzo's warm kiss. She'd felt it to the very marrow of her bones. If the doctor hadn't been in the room, she would have kissed him back and never stopped.

"If you recall, Michelina was the one who wanted me to live at the palace, but without her there, it will be better if I move back home with Dad until I have the baby." It was true she and Vincenzo felt too comfortable together. To her chagrin she knew his visits and plans involving her were a distraction that kept him from doing some of his normal functions. All of it needed to stop. A change of residence was the key.

His next comment surprised her. "I was going to suggest it after we got back from our cruise."

"I'm glad we're in agreement about that. I'll still be living on the grounds and can get room service whenever I want. Living with my father will put the kind of distance needed to ease the king's mind." To ease her own mind.

Abby had been thinking of the baby as *their* baby. When he'd kissed her after the sonogram, it had felt so right. She couldn't delude herself any longer. Abby was painfully in love with Vincenzo and felt as if his baby was her baby, too.

"In that case I'll ask some of my security people to move your things back this evening."

"I don't have anything except my clothes, really."

They'd reached the law firm. Vincenzo opened the door for her. She stepped outside, aware that the good news from the ultrasound had been swallowed up in the tension that had plagued them since Michelina's death.

"I'll see you this evening, Abby. Take care."

After putting in a full day's work, Vincenzo grabbed his phone and left for a run in the palace gym to work off his nervous energy. After a heavy workout, he returned to his suite to shower and shave. His phone rang while he was putting on a polo shirt over cargo pants. He'd asked the sentry guard to alert him when Abby got home from work.

Moving fast, he reached the door to her suite before she did. He wanted to catch her off guard. The second she came around the corner and saw him she stopped, causing the fetching green dress to wrap around her long legs for a moment.

"H-How long have you been waiting here?" Her voice faltered.

"Not more than a minute. I'll help you get packed and we'll have a last dinner here on your terrace. In a little while some of the security men will be here to take your things over."

"No, Vincenzo. I—"

"No?"

She looked conflicted. "What I meant to say is that I'm virtually halfway through this pregnancy and everything has gone fine so far. You don't need to wait on me hand and foot anymore!"

"I *want* to. There *is* a difference, you know. Since you're the only person on this planet who's going to make my dreams come true, would you deny me the privilege of showing my gratitude?"

"But you do it constantly."

He sucked in his breath. "Three-quarters of the time I've been out of the country or occupied with business, so that argument won't wash. All you have to do is tell me that you don't want my company and I'll stay away."

Her eyes flashed purple sparks. "I've always enjoyed your company, but—"

"But what?" he demanded.

"We talked about it in the limo. For the time being, it's best if you and I stay away from each other."

"Best for you, or for me?"

"Best for everyone! From the beginning we knew there'd be gossip. With Michelina's death everything has changed and I'm sure the king is wary of it. You have to know that, Vincenzo." Damn if she wasn't speaking truth. "My going back to live with Father will quiet a situation that's building, but you shouldn't be here helping."

"We've already covered that ground."

"And we'll keep covering it for as long as I'm underfoot here or on the royal yacht!" she cried.

"You *do* have a temper." He smiled. "This is the first time I've ever seen it."

Her face filled with color. "I…didn't mean to snap at you."

He gave an elegant shrug of his shoulders. "Instead of us standing around arguing, why don't you open the door and we'll get started on moving you—baggage and all—out of sight."

She drew closer to him. "Be reasonable."

"I'm offering my services to help. What's more reasonable than that?"

"Because it's not your job!"

The only person who'd ever dared talk to him like this was his father. Abby was even more alluring when she showed this side of her. "What do you think my job is? To sit on my golden throne all day long and order my subjects to fetch and carry for me?"

"*Yes!*"

But the minute she said it, he could tell she was embarrassed and he burst into laughter that filled the hallway. In another second she started laughing with him. "You're outrageous, Vincenzo."

"My mother used to tell me the same thing. Come on and let me in. After a workout in my golden gym, I'm dying for a cold lemonade."

"The door's open," she said in a quiet voice. "I only lock it at night, but there's really no need to do it, because you've assigned bodyguards who are as far away as my shadow."

CHAPTER SEVEN

VINCENZO OPENED THE door and waited for Abby to pass before he entered. But when he saw the sway of her hips, he had to fight the urge to wrap her in his arms and pull her body into him.

Never in his marriage with Michelina, let alone with the other women in his earlier years, had he known such an intense attack of desire, and without the slightest hint of provocation on Abby's part. She'd done nothing to bring out this response in him.

Somewhere along the way his feelings for her as a friend had turned into something entirely different. Perhaps it was the knowledge that she was leaving the palace tonight that had unleashed the carnal side of his nature. Maybe it was the reality of the baby now that he had the pictures in his possession, knowing it lived inside her body.

Her father was a red-blooded man who'd probably warned her ages ago not to go out on the yacht with him. Vincenzo's own father, a man with several quiet affairs in his background, had no doubt made it easy for Abby's father to leave his service to be certain no misstep was taken.

Vincenzo got it. He got it in spades. But the ache and longing for her had grown so acute, it actually frightened him.

While she was in her bedroom, he phoned the kitchen to have some sandwiches and salad brought up to the room. "This is Signorina Loretto's last evening in the palace. Tonight she's moving back to Signor Loretto's apartment on the grounds. You'll be delivering her meals there from now on when she requests them."

"Very good, Your Highness."

Having quieted that source of gossip for the moment, Vincenzo hung up and went looking for Abby. "I ordered some sandwiches to be brought. While we're waiting, what can I do to help?"

She had several suitcases on the bed and had already emptied her dresser drawers. "Well… there's not much to take. I left most of my things at Dad's. Maybe if you would empty my CDs and DVDs from the entertainment center. I'll clean out the things in the den myself. The men will have to bring some boxes to pack all my books and Michelina's paintings." She handed him an empty shoulder bag.

She had an impressive collection of operas, from *Madame Butterfly* to *Tosca.* Her choice of movies was as varied as the different traits of her personality. He packed all but one of them and went back to the bedroom. "You enjoyed this?"

Abby glanced at the cover. "*24?* I absolutely love that series. Have you seen it?"

"Yes, and I found it riveting from beginning to end."

Her eyes exploded with light. "Me, too! Did you see the series about the signing of the peace accord?" He nodded. "That was my favorite. Even my father thought it was good, and that's saying a lot considering the kind of work he's in. He only picked apart half of the things in it that bothered him."

A chuckle escaped Vincenzo's lips. "Shall we watch a few episodes of it tonight while we eat and direct traffic?"

"That sounds wonderful."

"Bene."

"Oh—someone's knocking."

"I'll get it."

He opened the door and set the dinner tray on the coffee table.

After she'd emptied the bathroom of her cosmetics, she started on the den. Abby worked fast and it didn't take long. "There!" She came back in the living room. "It's done. Now all your poor slaves can move everything to Dad's."

With a smile he told her to sit in the chair and put her feet up on the ottoman. It pleased him that he got no argument out of her. With a flick of the switch, he sat back on the couch and they began watching *24*.

Again it gratified him that she was hungry and ate her sandwich with more relish than usual. He'd been afraid their little scuffle in the hall had put her off her food, but it seemed that wasn't the case.

The thought came into his head that she was probably excited to live with her father again and enjoy his company. Which left Vincenzo nowhere.

He craved Abby's company. During his trip to France she was all he ever thought about. To his surprise, it wasn't because of the baby. Perhaps in the beginning the two had seemed inseparable, but no longer.

Abby was her own entity. Lovely, desirable. Her companionship brought him nothing but pleasure.

"Don't you think the queen is fantastic in this series? She was the perfect person to be cast in that part. How could the king want that other woman when he had a wife like her?" Abby was glued to the set. Vincenzo didn't think her remark was prompted by any other thought than the story itself, but it pressed his guilt button.

In his own way he'd been faithful to Michelina, but it hadn't been passionate love. This need for Abby had only come full force recently. His amorous feelings for her had crept up on him without his being aware.

"She's very beautiful in an exotic way," Vincenzo agreed, but his mind was elsewhere.

"How would it be to have been born that exotically beautiful? I can't even imagine it."

He slanted her a glance. "You have your own attributes. There's only one Abby Loretto."

"What a gentleman you are, Vincenzo. No wonder your subjects adore you."

"Abby—"

"No, no." She sat up straight. "Let me finish. All you have to do is look through that scrapbook again to see it."

A burst of anger flared inside him for his impossible situation.

"If you're trying to convince me to continue playing the role I was born to in life, it's not working. I'm no longer a baby who happened to be the child of a king. I've grown into a man with a man's needs. If I've shocked you once again, I'm sorry."

"I'm not a fool," she said quietly. "I can understand why you balk at the idea of marrying someone you don't love, even if it is your royal duty. After your experience with Michelina, it makes more sense than ever. But I can't believe that someday a woman with a royal background won't come along who sweeps you off your feet so you can take over for your father."

The program had ended. Abby got up from the chair to take the disk out of the machine and put it in the shoulder bag with the others.

He eyed her moodily. "Perhaps that miracle will occur. But we're getting ahead of ourselves. At this point, the birth of our child is the only event of importance in my life. It's all I can think about."

"That event isn't far off now."

No... He had less than six months before she left for the States. Getting to his feet he said, "The men should be here shortly. Come with me. If you're up to a walk, I'll escort you back to your old stomping grounds."

A happy laugh, like one from childhood, came out of her. "That sounds like a plan. I ate an extra sandwich half. The doctor would say that's a no-no. Otherwise at my next appointment I'll weigh in like—"

"Don't say it," he warned her. "I prefer my own vision of you."

She was turned away from him so he couldn't see her reaction. "I'll leave a note to tell them everything is here in the living room ready to go."

Vincenzo waited, then led her down another hall outside her apartment that came out at the side of the palace. They passed various staff as they walked down the steps and out the doors into an early evening.

July could be hot, but the breeze off the Mediterranean kept them cool enough to be comfortable. He'd crossed these grounds hundreds of times before, and many of those times with Abby. But this was different.

If he wasn't fearful of giving her a minor heart attack, he'd reach for her hand and hold it tight while they strolled through the gardens. Her father's apartment was in one of the outbuildings erected in the same style and structure as the palace. At one time it had housed certain members of the staff, but that was a century ago and it had since been renovated.

On impulse he stopped by a bed of hydrangea shrubs in full bloom to pick some flowers. "These are for you." He put them in her arms. "The petals are the color of your eyes. Not blue, not lavender, just somewhere in between."

"Their scent is heavenly." She buried her face in them, then lifted her head. "Thank you," she whispered. "You have no idea how many times over the years I've longed to pick these. Mother called them mop heads. These were her favorite flower and color."

"Maybe it's because she was reminded of them every time she looked into her only baby's eyes." Abby now averted them. "Abby, was there a reason your parents didn't have more children?"

She nodded. "Mom and Dad had me five years after they were married, because he'd been in the military. Two years later they decided to get pregnant again, but by that time Dad had been shot while on duty and it turned out he'd been rendered sterile. They weren't keen on adopting right away. I think it's one of the reasons they decided to move to Arancia, where they could make new memories."

Vincenzo was aghast. "I didn't know. Your father was so devastated when he lost her. I'll never forget."

"No. They were very much in love, but they had a great life all the same."

"And they had you." He was beginning to understand why she and her father were so close.

"Their inability to increase the family size was probably another motivating reason for my wanting to be a surrogate for you and Michelina. It's crazy, isn't it? So many women and men, whether in wedlock or not, seem to have little difficulty producing offspring while others..." Abby didn't finish the rest. She didn't have to.

They continued walking until they reached the apartment where she would live until the baby came. She left him long enough to put the flowers in water and bring the vase into the living room. He watched her look around after she'd set it on the coffee table.

This was the first time Vincenzo had been inside Carlo's suite. Family pictures were spread everywhere. He saw books and magazines her father must have read.

"Is it good to be home, Abby?"

She turned to him. "Yes and no. The apartment at the palace has been like home to me for quite a while. Both Dad and I can be semireclusive without meaning to be. We're both insatiable readers and like our privacy on occasion. He's going to have to put up with me invading his space again."

"Oh, I think he can handle it." Vincenzo happened to know her father had been on a countdown to get Abby out of the country from the time Michelina had died. "I'll stay until the men arrive with your things."

Abby sat down on one of the love seats, eyeing him with some anxiety. "I hope you didn't go to too much trouble to get the yacht ready."

"My father pays the captain a good salary to make certain it's able to sail at any time."

She shook her head. "I don't mean the money."

He let out a sigh. "I know you didn't. Frankly,

the only person put out is yours truly, because I had my heart set on taking you to Barcaggio, on the northern tip of Corsica."

"I've never been there. You think I'm not disappointed, too?"

Abby sounded as though she meant it. Her response went a long way toward calming the savage beast within him.

"With your love of history, you'd find it fascinating. They had a unique warning system, with sixty guard towers dating from the fifteenth century, to keep the island safe. At least three towers in sight of each other would light fires to give a warning signal of pirates approaching. The Tower of Barcaggio is one of the best conserved and the water around it is clear like the tropics."

"Don't tell me anything more or I'll go into a deep depression."

A rap on the door prevented him from responding. He was glad the men had come. The sooner they left, the sooner he could be alone with her for a while longer. "I'll answer it."

For the next few minutes, a line of security

people walked in with bags and boxes. Vincenzo helped to carry some of her law books into the library. What he saw on the desk gave him an idea. After he'd thanked them and they'd left, he called to Abby.

"Is there something wrong?" She hurried in, sounding a little out of breath.

"I think I've found a way we can be together for meals without leaving our suites."

She looked at him with those fabulous eyes. "How?"

"We'll coordinate our meals for the same time every evening and talk on Skype while we eat. That way I can check on you and know if you're lying when you tell me you're feeling fine."

Her lips twitched. "That works both ways. I'll know if you're in a mood."

"Exactly. Is it a deal?"

"Be serious, Vincenzo."

His heart beat skidded off the charts. "When I get back to my apartment, I'll Skype you to make sure everything's working properly."

"You don't mean every night?"

"Why not? Whether I'm away on business,

out of the country or in the palace, we both have to stop for food, and we're usually alone. At the end of a hectic day, I'd rather unwind with you than anyone else. It'll save me having to go through Angelina to find out your condition for the day. Shall we say seven?"

"That'll last about two minutes before you're called away to something you can't get out of."

He decided he'd better leave before her father showed up. Together they walked to the entrance of the apartment. "Shall we find out? How about we give this a thirty-day trial? That should keep the gossips quiet. Whoever misses will have to face the consequences."

Amusement lit up her eyes. "You're on, but a prince has so many commitments, methinks *you'll* be the one who will wish you hadn't started this."

Vincenzo opened the door. "Don't count on it. I'll be seeing you as soon as I get back to my apartment." He glanced at his watch. "Say, twenty minutes?"

"I won't believe it till I see you."

With that challenge, he left at a run for the

quick trip back to his suite. There was more than one way to storm the citadel for the rest of her pregnancy without physically touching her. He didn't dare touch her.

It disturbed him that though he'd been in a loveless marriage, he could fall for another woman this fast. He was actually shocked by the strength of his feelings. To get into a relationship was one thing, but for Abby to be the woman, Vincenzo needed to slow down so he wouldn't alarm her. He knew she was attracted to him. It wasn't something she could hide, but she never let herself go.

Because of her control, he had to hold back, but they couldn't exist teetering on the brink much longer. Thanks to cybertechnology, he'd found a way to assuage some of his guilt. Without others knowing, he could be with her every night for as long as he wanted to satisfy his need to see and talk to her while he focused on the baby.

Vincenzo intended to be a good father, but he was struggling with the fact that he'd fallen for the woman who was carrying his child. What did that say about him?

Abby hurriedly put away her clothes and got settled as best she could before heading for the library. Passing through the living room, she picked up the vase of flowers and carried it with her.

After putting it on the desk, she sat down at her dad's computer, ready to answer Vincenzo's call. The big screen rather than her laptop screen would be perfect to see him, *if* he did make contact. She didn't doubt his good intentions, but she knew from her father that the prince followed a tight schedule, one that often ran late into the evenings.

In her heart she knew the decision to move home had been the right one, but when Vincenzo had walked out the door a little while ago, a feeling of desolation swept through her. Her move from the palace had marked the end of the third journey. Now she was embarking on the fourth into the unknown and had the impression it would try her mettle.

She'd lost Michelina, who'd provided the interference. Now it was all on Vincenzo to support her, but he'd made the wise decision to stay at a distance. So had she, yet already she felt herself in free fall.

Trust that clever mind of his to dream up Skyping as a way to stay in touch without distressing their fathers or the queen. As she was coming to find out, Vincenzo's resourcefulness knew no bounds.

Unable to resist, she leaned over to smell the hydrangeas. She'd never see one again without remembering how he'd just stopped and picked an armload for her.

The way to a woman's heart… Vincenzo knew them all, she admitted to herself in an honest moment. He was in there so tightly, she was dying from the ache. There'd never be room for anyone else. The video-call tone rang out, making her jump.

"Good evening, Abby." She'd put the speaker on full volume to make certain she could hear him. The sound of his deep, velvety voice brought her out of her trancelike state.

His looks went beyond handsome. Adrenaline rushed through her veins. "Good evening, Your Highness."

"You've become very formal since I left you."

"I've got stage fright." It was the truth. No one in Arancia would believe what she was doing, and with whom.

"Our connection is good. We should have no problem communicating tomorrow evening."

"I might have one problem with the time. Dad is going to be home early for a dinner I'm cooking. Would you mind if we said eight-thirty?"

"I'll make a note on my agenda," he teased.

She smiled. "This is fun, Vincenzo."

"It's not the same as being with you in person, but I'm not complaining. Would you answer a question for me?"

"If I can."

"Did Dr. DeLuca let you know the gender of the baby?"

Her lungs froze. "No. He wanted to obey your wishes. I think you're wise not to know yet. Then your father and the queen would either be planning on a future king or future princess. This way everyone's still in the dark."

He chuckled. "I love the way you think, especially when you read my mind so easily. However, there is one thing I'm curious about. You never talk about the baby."

Pain stabbed at her heart. "I've been taking Dr. Greco's advice—don't think about the actual baby too much. Better to stay focused on taking care of yourself rather than dwelling on a child that won't be yours."

His face sobered. "How's that advice working out for you?"

She took a deep breath. "I'm finding it's very hard to carry out. I have to admit that if you hadn't asked me that question just now, I would know you had a stone for a heart."

"Abby," his voice grated, "you've accepted to do the impossible for me. You wouldn't be human if you weren't thinking about the baby day and night."

"You're right. During the talks I had with you and Michelina before I underwent the procedure, I made a decision to be like the postman who delivers the mail without knowing what's inside the letters.

"If a postman were to open one, he'd probably be so affected he would never make it to the next destination. Getting the ultrasound today was a lot like opening that first letter. I can't not think about the baby, whether it's a boy or a girl, if it will look like you or Michelina or someone else in your families."

Vincenzo turned solemn. "I've told you before, but I'll say it again. I'm in awe of you, Abby. You've taken on a weight too heavy to bear."

"You took on a weight, too. Not every man would trust a stranger with the life of his unborn child."

"You're no stranger," he answered in a smoky tone.

"You know what I mean."

"I don't think you know what *I* mean. You were never a stranger to me. A child in the beginning, of course, but from the beginning always a friend. I feel like I've known you all my life. It seemed a natural thing that you became our baby's surrogate mother."

She moistened her lips. "Depending on when the baby decides to come, we could be halfway home right now." Abby didn't want to think about the big event because of what it would mean. The thought of permanent separation was killing her. "Have you bought any things for the baby yet?"

"I'm glad you brought that up. In a few days I'm going to go shopping and would like your help to set up the well-furnished nursery."

He couldn't know how his comment thrilled her. "I'd love to be involved."

"I'll send you pictures online and we'll decide on things together."

"Do you know where you're putting the nursery?"

"Either in my apartment or the room down the hall next to it."

"What did Michelina want?"

"We never got that far in our thinking. Her concerns over telling Bianca about the pregnancy overshadowed the fun."

Of course. "Well, it's fun to think about it now. If it's in your apartment, you'll have a nanny coming and going out of your inner sanctum." His low chuckle thrilled her. "When you're up all hours of the night with a baby with colic, will you be glad it's near at hand or not?"

"I'll have to think on that one."

"While you do that, what's on your schedule for tomorrow?"

"You really don't want to know."

"Why don't you let *me* decide?"

His smile was wicked. "Remember that you asked. First I'll do a workout in the pool when I get up, then I'll get dressed and eat breakfast with my father, who will tell me what's on his mind. I'll scan a dozen or so newspapers on certain situations in the world.

"At ten I'll visit the Esposito social enterprise to meet the staff and disadvantaged young people working on a building project at Esposito Ricci.

"At eleven-thirty I'll meet representatives of the San Giovani Churches Trust, the National Churches Trust and restoration workers at Gallo-Conti.

"At noon I'll meet with the different faith communities at Gravina, where I'll be served lunch.

"At one-thirty, in my capacity as president of business, I'll visit the Hotel Domenico, which has been participating in my initiative to promote the meet-and-greet program in all the hotels. I'll visit the shop, which has been created in the meet-and-greet center, and chat with locals.

"At ten to three, as patron of the Toffoli Association, I'll meet staff and residents working at San Lucca Hospital. At four I'll meet pupils and staff at Chiatti Endowed Schools, where I'll tour the school hall and chapel. The pupils have prepared a brief performance for me.

"At ten to five I'll meet local community groups at the town hall in Cozza, as well as some members of the town council.

"At five-thirty, as president and founder of the Prince's Trust, I'll meet with young people who have participated in programs run by the trust, particularly the team program at the Moreno Hotel in Lanz."

Abby tried to take it in, but couldn't. "You made that up."

He crossed himself. "I swear I didn't."

"You mean that's all? That's it? You didn't have time to ride around in your made-for-the-prince sports car?" she exclaimed. "You're right, Vincenzo. I really didn't want to know and never want to think about it again."

Coming over the Skype, his laughter was so infectious she laughed until she had tears, which was how her father found her when he walked in the den. He could see Vincenzo in all his glory on the screen.

"Abby? Why aren't you talking?"

Her father had leaned over to smell the hydrangeas. "I have company."

Vincenzo didn't blink an eye. "Tell your father good evening."

"I will. *Buonanotte,* Your Highness."

She turned off the Skype. Nervous, she looked over at her dad, who had the strangest look on his face.

"Guilio told me his son has always been perfectly behaved. I wonder what could have happened to him."

Abby got up from the desk, needing to think of something quick. "He's going to be a father."

Carlo gave her a hug. "That must be the reason. Welcome home, sweetheart."

CHAPTER EIGHT

Reporters besieged Abby as she and Signor Giordano came out of the Palazzo di Giustizia in downtown Arancia. She'd won the case for him and it meant some big changes for the country's trade policies. Judge Mascotti had summoned her to the bench after announcing his ruling.

"I realize the palace was interested in this case, but I want you to know I made my decision based on the merits you presented."

Abby couldn't have been more pleased to hear those words.

For court she'd pulled her hair back to her nape and used pins to hold a few coils in place.

She'd worn a navy designer maternity outfit with a smart white jacket. The dress draped from a high waistline and fell to the knee. Her bump seemed quite big to her already, but the jacket camouflaged it well. On her feet she wore strappy white sandals.

Mid-August meant she was into her twenty-third week of pregnancy. Two days ago she'd had her first episode of Braxton-Hicks contractions, but the doctor said it was normal because her body was getting ready. When Vincenzo found out, he had a talk with Dr. DeLuca and they both decided she should quit work.

Abby wasn't ready to stay home yet. Without work to do she'd go crazy, but she'd made an agreement in the beginning and had to honor it. When she got back to her office there was a celebration with champagne, not only because this case was important to their firm, but because it was her last day at work.

Everyone thought she was going back to the States, so she let them think it. Carolena poured white grape juice into her champagne glass when no one was looking. That was how she got through the party. If some of them realized she was pregnant, no one said anything.

After Skyping with Vincenzo every night from the start, except for the night she'd gone to the hospital about her false contractions, she told Carolena to Skype her at the apartment. Until the birth of the baby, Abby planned to do research for her friend to help pass the time. Carolena had a backlog of work and had gone crazy over the idea.

They drank to their plan and Abby left the office in brighter spirits than before. She walked out to the limo pretty much depleted energy-wise after her court appearance. Once settled inside, she rested her head against the back of the seat and closed her eyes, still thinking about what the judge had said to her.

She worked hard on every case, but that one had special meaning because it would benefit Arancia. After listening to Vincenzo's schedule for one day, she realized he'd spent his whole adult life promoting the welfare of his country. It felt good to know she'd made a tiny contribution toward his goals.

"Signorina?" She opened her eyes to discover they'd arrived at the harbor. "Your presence is requested aboard the yacht. If you'll step this way, please."

Her heart thundered in her chest as she climbed out and walked with a security man up the gangplank into the gleaming white royal craft. Angelina was there to meet her.

"The palace heard of your victory in court and wishes to honor you with an overnight cruise. A few of your personal things are on board. Come with me and I'll show you to your cabin. Your orders are to relax, swim, eat and wander the deck at will."

"Thanks, Angelina," she murmured, too overcome to manage any more words and followed her. Strange as it was, this meant she'd miss her nightly conversation with Vincenzo. How crazy was that, when anyone else would be jumping out of their skin with joy at such a privilege?

But she'd lived on the palace grounds for years and inside the palace for four months of that time. She'd learned that if Vincenzo wasn't there, it didn't matter if the whole place was paved in gold. Since the judge's ruling, she'd been living to talk to him about everything tonight. Now she'd have to wait until tomorrow night.

"Is there anything else I can do for you?" Angelina asked from the doorway. The separate cabins were on the main deck, with a glorious view of the sea.

"I'm fine, thanks. Right now I just want to lie down. It's been a long day." She checked her watch. Five to six.

"Of course. If you need something, pick up the phone and the person on the other end will contact me. There's food and drink already on the table for you."

She nodded and closed the door after her. The queen-size bed looked good. After closing the shutters over the windows, Abby went to the bathroom, then removed her jacket and sandals. She ate half her club sandwich and some fruit salad before walking over to the bed. She'd undress all the way later. For the moment she was too tired to take off the sleeveless dress before she simply lay down to close her eyes for a little while.

The last thing Abby remembered before she lost consciousness was the movement of the yacht. When she heard someone calling her name, she thought it was the prince talking to her through Skype. She stirred.

"Vincenzo?"

"I'm right here."

"Oh, good. I wanted to talk to you and was afraid we wouldn't be able to until tomorrow night." But as she sat up in the semidark room, she realized something wasn't right. Abby wasn't at the desk. She was on the yacht and there was Vincenzo standing right in front of her in jeans and a sport shirt.

Her pulse raced. "You're here! I mean, you're *really* here."

"I knocked, but you didn't hear me, so I came in the room to check up on you. You didn't eat a lot of the dinner Angelina brought in."

"I was too tired to eat very much when I reached the room." Abby's hair had come unpinned and fell around her shoulders. "How did you get here?"

"I flew aboard on the helicopter. Are you all right?"

No. She wasn't! Abby hadn't seen him in person in about six weeks. The shock was too much and she was totally disoriented.

"Abby?" he prodded.

"Yes," she said too loudly, sounding cross. He was much too close. She smoothed the hair out of her eyes. "You're not supposed to be here."

"Don't get up," he admonished gently, but she felt at a disadvantage sitting there and stood up anyway. "You're the loser in our contest, remember? This is the penalty I've chosen to inflict, so you're stuck with me until morning."

Her body couldn't stop trembling. "I confess I didn't think you could stick to it."

"Is that all you have to say?"

She'd been caught off guard and didn't know if she could handle this. A whole night together? "What do you want me to say?"

"That you're happy to see me."

"Well, of course I am." But the words came out grouchy.

"You really do look pregnant now. Will you let me feel you?"

If he'd shot her, she couldn't have been more astonished. That's why he kept standing there? It was a perfectly understandable request. It was his baby, after all. But this was one time when she didn't know what to do. To say no to him didn't seem right. But to say yes…

On instinct she reached for his hand and put it on her bump, to make it easier for both of them. It wasn't as if he hadn't touched her before. Heavens, he'd saved her life. She'd sobbed in his arms.

But there had been a whole new situation since then. The warmth of his fingers seeped through the material of her dress, sending a charge of electricity through her body. She held her breath while he explored.

"Have you felt it move?" he asked in a husky voice.

"I've had quickenings, kind of like flutters. At first I wasn't sure. They only started a few days ago. But when I lay down a few hours ago, I felt a definite movement and knew it wasn't hunger pains."

"It's miraculous, isn't it?" His face was so close to hers, she could feel his breath on her cheek. He kept feeling, shaping his hand against her swollen belly. "I'm glad you're through working and can stay home, where you and the baby are safe."

She bowed her head. "No place is perfectly safe, Vincenzo."

"True, but you were on television today in front of the courthouse. I saw all those steps and a vision of you falling. It ruined the segment for me."

"Signor Giordano had hold of my arm."

"I noticed. He's recently divorced from his wife."

How did Vincenzo know that? But the minute she asked herself the question, she realized how foolish she was. He always checked out everything she did and everyone she worked with.

"I found him very nice and very committed to his fast-track proposal."

"Has he asked you to go out with him?"

Why did Vincenzo want to know? It couldn't be of any importance to him. "He did when he put me in the limo."

His hand stopped roving. "What did you tell him?"

"What I told everyone at my goodbye party.

I'm moving back to the States." If she said it long and hard enough, she'd believe it, but his tension heightened. Being barefoot, Abby felt shorter next to his well-honed physique. She took the opportunity to ease away from him before turning on the switch that lit the lamps on either side of the bed.

He gazed at her across the expanse. "Are you still exhausted?"

No. His exploration of her belly had brought her senses alive and no doubt had raised her blood pressure. If he was asking her if she wanted to go up on deck and enjoy the night, the answer was yes. But she could hear her father saying, "I wouldn't advise it."

They'd both crossed a line tonight. His wish to feel the baby was one thing, but she'd sensed his desire for her. Since her own desire for him had been steadily growing for months, there was no point in denying its existence. Once you felt its power and knew what it was, all the excuses in the world couldn't take that knowledge away. Could you die of guilt? She wondered…

But to give in to it to satisfy a carnal urge

would cheapen the gift. She'd told the queen this was a sacred trust. So she smiled at him.

"Maybe not exhausted, but pleasantly tired. I need a shower and then plan to turn in. Why don't we have breakfast in the morning on deck and enjoy a swim? That I would love." *Keep him away from you, Abby.*

"We'll be along the coast of Corsica at dawn. If you're up by seven-thirty, you'll see the water at its clearest."

Part of her had been hoping he'd tell her he didn't want her to go to bed yet, but he was a highly principled man and had made a promise to get her safely through this experience. "I'll set my alarm for that time and join you."

"Good night, then." As Vincenzo turned to leave she called his name.

"Thank you for this unexpected surprise."

"You won the court case and deserve a treat. Everyone in the country will benefit."

"Thank you. But I'm talking about more than a night on this fabulous yacht. I want to thank you for our nightly video sessions. I looked forward to every one of them."

His brows lifted. "They're not over."

"I'm so glad to hear that."

"They've saved my life, too, Abby." On that confession, he left her cabin and shut the door.

To read more into those words would be Abby's downfall. They were both waiting out this pregnancy on tenterhooks in a cage no one else could see. It was an unnatural time under the most unnatural circumstances a prince and a commoner could be in. The closer they got to the delivery date, the more amazed she was that she and Vincenzo had made things work this far.

During the early-morning hours, the sun burned a hole through clouds over the Mediterranean. The ray of light penetrated the turquoise water near the guard tower he'd told her about. Abby had thrown on a beach robe and leaned over the yacht's railing to see how far down it went, causing her braid to dangle.

Vincenzo had done several dives and wore his black trunks, so she could see his hard-muscled body clearly. The dramatically rugged landscape continued underwater in the form of more mountains, canyons, needles, peaks and rocky masses. He clung to some huge rocks below the waterline, then moved downward until he was almost out of sight.

Though he swam like a fish, she was nervous until she saw him come up for air. Abby wished she'd brought a camera to capture him on film, but when she'd left the courthouse yesterday, she could never have imagined where she'd end up.

"I'm envious of you!" she shouted to him. Even though it was August, she'd bet the water was cold this morning, but he seemed impervious to any discomfort.

"One day soon you'll be able to do this," he called back to her.

Not this. Not here. Not with him.

"Is there anything dangerous lurking down there?"

"Only a big white."

"Vincenzo!"

A grin appeared on his striking face. With his black hair slicked back, he was the stuff women's fantasies were made of. "Is breakfast ready?"

She giggled. "Have I told you how funny you are sometimes? You know very well your food is always ready!"

"Well, I'm starving!"

"So am I!"

He swam with expertise to the transom of the fifty-two-foot luxury yacht and came aboard. In a minute they were seated around the pool being served a fantastic meal. Once they'd eaten, Abby took off her robe to sunbathe for a little while. Their loungers were placed side by side. Talk about heaven!

The yacht was moving again, this time around the island. By tomorrow evening her idyll would be over, but she refused to think about that yet.

After the intimacy they'd shared last night when he'd reached out to feel the baby, she decided it didn't matter that he could see her pregnant with only her bikini on. Those black eyes slid over her from time to time, but he never made her feel uncomfortable.

The deck steward brought them reading material in case they wanted it. Vincenzo propped himself on one elbow to scan the newspaper. "You made the front page yesterday. I quote, 'A new star has risen in the legal firmament of Arancia.

"'One might take her for a film star, but Signorina Abigail Loretto, a stunning blonde with the law firm of Faustino, Ruggeri, Duomo and Tonelli, has a brain and pulled off a coup for import trade in Judge Mascotti's court that had the attorney for Signor Masala already filing an appeal.'"

Vincenzo handed it to her so she could have a look. "Have I told you how proud I am of you?"

Her body filled with warmth that had nothing to do with the sun. "Am I lying here on the royal yacht being treated like a princess by none other than His Royal Highness?"

"I think we need to start a scrapbook for you."

"It will be a pitiful one, since I quit work yesterday. This was it. My one meteoric rise to fame that came and went in a flash. I hope it's all right with you if I help do research for Carolena at the apartment."

"Your life is your own, Abby. My only concern is that you keep your stress level to a minimum, for your sake as well as the baby's."

"Agreed."

His eyes played over her. "You're picking up a lot of sun, but it's hard to feel it with the breeze."

"You're right. I'll cover up in a minute."

"Abby—" She could tell he had something serious on his mind.

"What is it?"

"When you hear what I have to tell you, it will cause you some stress, but it has to be said."

"Go on."

"We've told Gianna about the situation."

Alarmed, she sat up in the lounger and reached for the beach towel to throw over her. "How long has she known?"

"My sister saw you on the evening news. Since she's known you for years, too, she phoned me about it. I was with Father when her call came through. Now that you've been identified to the public, so to speak, we decided it was time she knew about the baby in case word got out and she hadn't heard it first."

"That makes sense, Vincenzo. She'd be hurt if you hadn't told her." Her heart pounded so hard, it was painful. "Did she have the same reaction as your mother-in-law?"

He sat up to talk. "No. She thinks it's terribly modern of all of us—her exact words—but couldn't believe Michelina would go along with the idea."

"Because of the queen?"

"No," he murmured, sounding far away. Abby supposed she knew the real answer deep down.

"Then it was because *I'm* the surrogate."

Vincenzo's silence for the next minute told its own tale. "It's nothing personal," he said in a grating voice.

"I know that."

"She's afraid of how it's going to look when the news gets out. You and I have already discussed this at length, but I wanted you to be prepared when she and her husband come for a visit."

"How soon?"

"Tonight."

Abby's breath caught.

"If she weren't coming, we could have stayed out another night. You don't have to meet with her if you don't want to, Abby. This is none of her business."

"But it is, Vincenzo. She's going to be your baby's aunt. We'll face her together like we faced the queen. Was she good friends with Michelina?"

He nodded. "They were very close. I know for a fact Gianna's hurt because Michelina never confided in her about this."

"Some matters aren't for anyone's ears except your own spouse. Surely she understands that."

"You would think so." He threw a towel around his shoulders and got up from the lounger. "Come on. You need to get out of the sun."

She pulled on her robe and they walked to the covered bar laid out with cocktail tables and padded chairs. Soft rock played through the speakers. One of the stewards brought them iced lime drinks.

"I'm sorry your sister is upset, but I'm not worried about it, if that's what you're thinking.

I had my trial of fire with the queen." A smile slowly broke from her.

Vincenzo saw it and covered her free hand with his own. "Then I won't take on that worry." He squeezed it, then let her go with reluctance and sat back. But she still felt the warmth and pressure of his after it had been removed.

"How long will it take us to get back to port?"

"For you, about five hours."

She groaned inside. "But not you."

"No. Another helicopter will be arriving in a half hour to take me back." The yacht had everything, including a landing pad. "Before I leave, I want to dance with you."

Ignoring her slight gasp, he reached for her and drew her into his arms. He moved them around slowly, pressing her against him.

"Do you know how incredible it is to be holding you in my arms while our baby is nestled right here between us?"

Abby couldn't breathe.

"I've needed to feel you like this for a long time. Don't fight me, Abby." He kissed her cheek and neck, her hair.

She felt as if she would faint from ecstasy. The last thing she wanted to do was push him away. For a little while she let herself go and clung to him. "I wish you didn't have to leave," she whispered.

"It's the last thing I want to do." While she was trying to recover from her severe disappointment that he had to go, he brushed his lips against hers before giving her a man's kiss, hot with desire. It spiked through her like electricity.

Close to a faint, she heard the sound of rotors and saw a speck in the sky coming their way. As it grew larger, she felt her heart being chopped into little pieces. Vincenzo had given her a fantastic surprise, but she wished he hadn't. She couldn't handle being around him like this and being kissed like this, only for him to be whisked away. This was torture.

"I'm afraid it will be better if no one sees us arriving together. The paparazzi will be out in full force. Angelina's going to help you leave with some of the staff from the yacht."

"You've had to go to a lot of trouble for me."

"How could it possibly compare with what you're doing for me?" She averted her eyes. "I'll send for you when it's time. We'll meet in the state drawing room as before. It's the only neutral ground in the palace, if you understand my meaning."

She knew what he meant. They couldn't talk to his sister in either of their apartments or his father's.

Though it was painful, she slowly eased out of his arms. "You need to get ready to go, so I'll say goodbye now and take a shower in my cabin."

He moved fast and accompanied her along the deck to open the door for her. But when she went inside and started to shut it, he stood there so she couldn't. His eyes stared at her. The desire in those black depths was unmistakable. She went weak at the knees. A small nerve throbbed at the corner of the mouth she was dying to taste over and over again.

"I'll see you tonight," he whispered in a raw-sounding voice she hardly recognized.

"Stay safe, Vincenzo. Don't let anything happen to you in that helicopter. Your child's going to need you."

"Abby—the last thing I want to do is leave you."

Then don't! she wanted to cry out. "With family coming, you have to."

His face darkened with lines. "Promise me you won't let Gianna get to you."

"She couldn't."

Abby had the feeling he wanted to warn her about something, then changed his mind.

"It'll be all right, Vincenzo."

His jaw hardened. "I'll Skype you at ten tonight."

She'd be living for it. *"A presto."*

Abby shut the door. After the passion in that kiss, this time it had to be goodbye for good.

When Marcello ushered Abby, wearing her jacketed white dress with the brown trim, into the drawing room, she glowed from the sun she'd picked up on her one day cruise. Her blond hair had been caught back with a dark comb. The newspaper had been right. She was stunning. Vincenzo had never seen her looking so beautiful.

"Gianna and I are glad you're here, Abby," he said, welcoming her to come in and sit down.

"I am, too. It's wonderful to see you again, Gianna." Since they'd all known each other for years, Vincenzo had dispensed with the pretense of formality, hoping to put Abby at ease. But he needn't have worried. She had incredible poise. Her self-possession came naturally to her and served her well in her profession.

Gianna, a tall brunette, smiled at her. "Pregnancy becomes you. You look well."

Vincenzo cringed. His sister wasn't pregnant yet and had gone straight for the jugular. So far the two women in his life who'd insisted on talking to Abby since Michelina's death had managed to show a side that couldn't help but hurt her, though she would deny it.

"Thank you. I feel fine."

His sister crossed her slim legs. "I told Vincenzo I wanted a private word with you. Do you mind?"

"Of course not."

He took that as his cue. "I'll be outside," he told Abby before leaving the room. For the next ten minutes he paced before she came out of the double doors. Despite her newly acquired tan, she'd lost a little color. He was furious with Gianna, but since their father had insisted she be allowed to talk with Abby, Vincenzo had given in, knowing it wouldn't go well.

"Are you all right?"

"I'm fine."

"I'll walk you back to your father's apartment."

"Please don't." It was the first time in their lives she'd ever spoken to him in a cold tone. Gianna had to have been brutal.

"I'll call you as soon as I know you're home." When Abby didn't respond he said, "We have to talk. I want your promise that you'll answer, otherwise I'll show up at your door."

"I—I need to go." Her voice faltered before she hurried down the hall and disappeared around the corner.

Tamping down his fury, he went back inside the drawing room. Gianna was waiting for him.

He knew that look. "What in the hell did you say to her?"

Ten minutes later he started for the doors.

"Don't you dare walk out on me!"

Vincenzo wheeled around. "I already did." He strode rapidly through the corridors to the east entrance of the palace and raced across the grounds to Carlo's apartment. Once he arrived, he knocked on the door and didn't stop until Abby answered. After closing the door, he took one glance at her wan face and pulled her into his arms.

"Gianna told me what she unleashed on you. I'm so sorry." He cupped the back of her head and pressed it into his shoulder, kissing her hair. "You have to know it was her pain talking. She had to marry a man she didn't love and so far she hasn't conceived. Though she's attractive, she's not a beauty like you and never was. Her jealousy of you and your association with Michelina finally reared its ugly head."

It was like déjà vu with Abby sobbing quietly against him, the way she'd done after she'd been rescued.

"She used scare tactics on you so you'll leave, but don't you know I'd never let you go?"

After she went quiet, she pulled away from him. Her eyes resembled drenched violets. "Maybe I should."

"Abby—how can you even say that?"

She stared at him, looking broken. "The issues she brought up I've already faced in my mind, except for one."

"Which one?"

"Your child. The thought of it growing up with doubts about who its mother really is breaks my heart."

Vincenzo didn't think he could ever forgive Gianna for planting that absurd fear in Abby's mind. "The baby will be a part of Michelina. Michelina had distinctive genes, like her mother and brother. They don't lie, remember?"

She took a shuddering breath. "You're right. How silly of me."

"Not silly, only human in the face of behavior I haven't seen come out of my sister since she was a teenager and threw a tantrum because she couldn't get her own way. But she'll calm down in time, just like the queen. I left her with the prospect that when Father steps down, she'll be the new ruler of Arancia.

"As Dr. DeLuca reminded us, this is a nine-day wonder that will be over for her soon. The good news is, you've walked through your last fire. From now on, we wait until our baby sends you into labor. Does the prospect make you nervous?"

She nodded and put on a smile for him. "Yes, but I'm not frightened, exactly. How could I be, when hundreds of thousands of babies are born every day? It's just that this baby is special."

"After finding out what it's like to be an expectant father, I've learned every baby is special if it's yours, royal or not. If Gianna had given me the chance, I would have told her you've been a blessing to Michelina and me. She would say the same thing if she were here, so never forget it."

"I won't."

"Do you believe me, Abby? It's imperative you believe it."

Her eyes searched his. "Of course I do."

"Thank you for that." Without conscious thought, he brushed his lips against hers. "I have to go and we'll see each other tomorrow night at seven o'clock. Right?"

"Yes."

Before he went back to the palace, he hurried down to their private beach. After ripping off his clothes, he lunged into the water and swam until he had no more strength before returning to his suite.

His phone registered four messages, from Marcello, his father, Gianna, and Gianna's husband, Enzio.

Not tonight.

Normally he didn't drink except on certain occasions. But right now he needed one or he'd never get to sleep. However, even the alcohol couldn't quiet the adrenaline gushing through his system since he'd held Abby. He'd felt every curve of her body.

Tonight he'd felt the baby move against him, igniting a spark that brought him to life in a brand-new way. It was something he'd never expected to feel. The last thing he remembered before oblivion took over was the sweet, innocent taste of her lips. *Abby, Abby.*

CHAPTER NINE

WHEN ABBY COULDN'T reach her father, she left him a message.

"Hi, Dad. I'm just leaving the doctor's office and wanted to report that my checkup went fine. Can you believe my pregnancy is almost over? I'm meeting Carolena for dinner at Emilio's, then we're going to the concert hall to see Aida. Be sure and eat your dinner. It's in the fridge."

This was one night she wouldn't be Skyping with Vincenzo. Last night she'd told him her plans. He wasn't too happy about her sitting through an opera all evening, but she promised to take it easy during the day.

Since the night when everything had come to a head because of Gianna, he hadn't surprised her by showing up unexpectedly. For the last little while he'd been treating her like a friend. She was doing the same. No contact except for technology. It was much easier this way and relieved her of a lot of guilt.

Gianna had forced Abby to face up to the fact that she was desperately in love with Vincenzo. When he'd kissed her before leaving the apartment, it had taken every ounce of her will not to return it. That kiss from him had been one of affection, not passion. It was his way of trying to comfort her.

She loved him for it.

She loved him to the depth of her soul.

During the last scene of *Aida,* she came close to falling apart. Radamès had been taken into the lower part of the temple to be sealed in a dark vault. Aida was hidden there so she could die with him.

When the tenor cried that he'd never see the light of day again, never see Aida again, she told him she was there to die with him. As they fell into each other's arms, Abby choked up. Tears dripped off her chin onto her program because she could imagine a love like that. It was the way she felt about Vincenzo. Before long she'd have the baby and then she'd be gone

for good. Thinking of that goodbye was excru-
ciating.

On the way home in the limousine, Carolena
teased her that she was full of hormones. Abby
attributed her breakdown to the glorious music
and voices, but they both knew it was much
more than that.

Her dad was at the computer when she walked
in the apartment. He lifted his head. "How was
the opera?"

"Fantastic."

"You look like you've been crying."

She smiled at him. "Come on, Dad. You know
Aida is a real tearjerker." They both loved opera.

"Your aunt phoned me today. They've found
a house for us near them and sent an email with
pictures. Take a look and see what you think. I
like it more than any of the others she's sent."

Abby wandered over and stood next to him
to check it out. "That's a darling house. I love
the Cape Cod style. Let's do it."

Her response seemed to satisfy him. He
turned to look at her. "Did you tell Dr. DeLuca
about our plans?"

"Yes. He says he has no problem about my flying back to the States within a week of the delivery, provided I'm not having complications. Since Vincenzo is having us flown on the royal jet with a doctor on standby, Dr. DeLuca is fine with it."

"Good."

"He told me something else. Though he hopes I'll go full-term, I shouldn't worry if I start into labor sooner. The baby has dropped and could be born any time now. He says it would be fine. I was glad for that reassurance. My pregnancy has been so free of problems, it's comforting to know that if there's a complication now, the baby will be all right."

"That reassures me, too."

"Dad? Are you having second thoughts about leaving Arancia?"

Their gazes connected. "Absolutely not. There comes a time when you know you're done. How about you?"

"Naturally I'm going to miss it. I've spent more than half my life here, but we have family in Rhode Island and you'll be there. Once

I'm settled in a law practice and take the bar, I know I'll be happy."

"I do, too. You'd better get to bed now, honey."

"I'm going. Good night." She kissed his forehead and left for her bedroom.

While she got ready, her mind was on her father. Abby knew he'd had relationships with several women since her mother died, but he seemed eager to leave Arancia. Since she didn't think it was all because of the situation with Vincenzo, she wondered if there was someone back home he'd known before and was anxious to see again.

Once she got under the covers, there was no comfortable position anymore. Then she got hot and threw them off. She'd had backache for the last week and looked like that beached whale. The doctor said she was a good size. Though she'd tried not to think about having to give up the baby, it had kicked her a lot since her sixth month and made her wonder if it was a boy with Vincenzo's great legs.

Abby knew he would have loved to feel it kicking, but by tacit agreement they'd stayed away from each other. She went swimming when he didn't. He didn't pick her up in the limo. Being able to Skype made it possible for them to talk to each other face-to-face and design the nursery, but that was it. Those days would soon be over.

Everything was planned out. Once Abby delivered, she'd be taken to a private place away from any staff or media before the flight back to the States. The contract she'd made in the beginning was specific: no contact with the baby or the parents. Abby's job would be done. That would be it, the end of her association with Vincenzo.

No meetings, no Skyping, no technology to connect them. It had to be that way for the rest of their lives, for the good of the kingdom, for all of them. Vincenzo would be the prince she couldn't forget, but he could never be a part of her life again.

Carolena was getting ready to go to court with a big law case. The work she'd asked Abby to do while she waited out these last few weeks was heaven-sent. Every time she started thinking about the little life getting ready to come into the world, she'd get busy doing more research. But she couldn't turn off her mind in the middle of the night.

Like Vincenzo, this child would be born into that world never knowing anything else. He'd make a marvelous father. She was excited for him, because his whole world was going to change once the doctor put the baby in his arms.

But to never see the baby, to never see Vincenzo again. She sobbed until oblivion took over.

Dr. DeLuca had given her the phone numbers of several former surrogates, but she hadn't felt the need to talk to them. No matter what, every surrogate's experience giving up a baby was different. Hers most of all, since she loved this royal heir and its father with every fiber of her being.

About five in the morning she woke up with lower-back pain. This was a little stronger than usual. She knew it could mean the onset of labor. Then again, it might be because she'd been to the opera last evening and it had been too much for her poor back.

She went to the bathroom and walked around the apartment for a few minutes. The ache subsided. Instead of going back to bed, she sat on the couch with her legs outstretched to watch a Godzilla film in Italian. Her feet were swollen. So were her fingers.

The film put her to sleep, but pain woke her up again. Whoa. She got up to go to the bathroom. Um. It hurt. It hurt a lot.

She went into her father's bedroom. "Dad? Did Mom have a bad backache before I came?"

He shot up in bed. "She sure did. The pain came around to the front."

"Yup. That's what I've got."

"I'll call the doctor."

"Tell him not to alert Vincenzo and tell him no one at the hospital is to leak this to him on the threat of death!"

"You can't ask him that, honey."

"Yes, I can!" She yelled at him for the first time in her life. "I'm the one having this baby and I'm not Vincenzo's wife. This isn't my child." Tears rolled down her hot cheeks. "If something goes wrong, I don't want him there until it's all over. He's been through enough suffering in his life. If everything's fine, then he ca— O-o-h. Wow. That was a sharp pain.

"Dad? Promise me you'll tell the doctor exactly what I said! I've been good about everything, but I want my way in this one thing!

"And make Angelina swear to keep quiet. If she breathes one word of this to Vincenzo, then—oh, my gosh—you'll fire her without pay and she'll never get another job for as long as she lives. I'm depending on you, Dad. Don't let me down."

He put a hand on her cheek. "Honey, I promise to take care of everything." Then he pressed the digit on his phone.

Vincenzo's life had become a ritual of staying alive to hear about Abby's day, but he was slowly losing his mind.

After a grueling session with parliament, he hurried to his apartment for a shower, then rang for some sandwiches and headed for the computer. It was time for his nightly call to Abby. With the baby's time coming soon, he couldn't settle down to anything. The only moments of peace were when he could see her and they'd talk.

Tonight he was surprised because he had to wait for her to tune in. One minute grew to two, then five. He gave her another five in case she was held up. Still no response.

The phone rang. It was Angelina. He broke out in a cold sweat, sensing something was wrong before he clicked on. "Angelina?"

"I wasn't supposed to let you know, but I think you have the right. You're about to become a father, Vincenzo."

What? "Isn't it too soon?"

"Not according to Abby's timetable. She didn't want you to worry, so she didn't want you to come to the hospital until after the delivery, but I know you want to be there. The limo is waiting downstairs to take you to the hospital."

His heart gave a great thump. "I owe you, Angelina! I'm on my way down."

Vincenzo flew out of the apartment and reached the entrance in record time. "Giovanni? Take me to the hospital, stat!"

Everything became a big blur before one of his security men said, "Come this way, Vincenzo." They took the elevator to the fourth floor, past the nursery to one of the rooms in the maternity wing.

"When did she go into labor?"

"Awhile ago," came the vague response. Vincenzo wanted to know more, but a nurse appeared and told him to wash his hands. Then she put a mask and gown on him before helping him into plastic gloves. He couldn't believe this was finally happening.

"Wait here."

As she opened the door, he saw Dr. DeLuca working with Abby. He was telling her to push. His beautiful Abby was struggling with all her might. "Push again, Abby."

"I'm trying, but I can't do this alone. I need Vincenzo. Where is he?" Her cry rang in the air. "I want him here!"

That was all Vincenzo needed to hear. He hurried into the operating room. The doctor saw him and nodded. "He's arrived."

"I'm here, Abby."

She turned her head. "Vincenzo!" He heard joy in her voice. "Our baby's coming! I should have called you."

"I'm here now. Keep pushing. You can do it."

After she pushed for another ten minutes, before his very eyes he saw the baby emerge and heard the gurgle before it let out a cry. Dr. DeLuca lifted it in the air. "Congratulations, Abby and Vincenzo. You have a beautiful boy." He laid the baby across her stomach and cut the cord.

"A *son,* Vincenzo!" Abby was sobbing for joy. "We did it."

"No, you did it." He leaned over and brushed her mouth.

The staff took over to clean the baby. In a minute the pediatrician announced, "The next heir to the throne is seven pounds, twenty-two inches long and looks perfect!"

He brought the bundled baby over and would

have placed it in his arms, but Vincenzo said, "Let Abby hold him first."

The moment was surreal for Vincenzo as together they looked down into the face of the child he and Michelina had created, the child Abby had carried. His heart melted at the sight.

"*Buonasera,* Maximilliano," she said with tears running down her cheeks. "Oh, he's so adorable."

Vincenzo could only agree. He leaned down to kiss the baby's cheeks and finger the dark hair. Carefully he unwrapped their little Max, who *was* perfect, with Michelina's eyes and ears.

"Look, Vincenzo. He has your jaw and the Di Laurentis body shape."

All the parts and pieces were there in all the right places. Vincenzo was overwhelmed.

Dr. DeLuca patted his shoulder. "You should go with the pediatrician, who's taking the baby to the nursery. I need to take care of Abby."

"All right." He leaned down again, this time to kiss her hot cheek. "I'll be back."

* * *

An hour later he left the nursery to be with Abby, but was told she was still in recovery. He could wait in the anteroom until she was ready to be moved to a private room. But the wait turned out to be too long and he knew something was terribly wrong.

He hurried to the nursing station. "Where's Signorina Loretto?" He was desperate to see the woman who'd made all this possible. She'd done all the work. She and the baby were inseparable in his mind and heart.

"She's not here, Vincenzo." Dr. DeLuca's voice.

He spun around. "What do you mean? To hell with the agreement, Doctor!"

Vincenzo felt another squeeze on his shoulder and looked up into Carlo's eyes staring at him above the mask he'd put on. "We all knew this was going to be the hard part. Abby's out of your life now, remember?

"Your boy needs you. Concentrate on him. You have all the help you need and a kingdom waiting to hear the marvelous news about the young prince, especially this bambino's grandfather and grandmother."

Vincenzo didn't feel complete without her. "Where is she, Carlo?"

"Asleep. She had back pain around five in the morning. In total she was in labor about fifteen hours. All went well and now that the delivery is over, she's doing fine."

"Tell me where she is," Vincenzo demanded.

"For her protection as well as yours, she's in a safe place to avoid the media."

He felt the onset of rage. "You mean she's been put in a witness protection program?"

"Of a sort. She fulfilled her part of the bargain to the letter and is in excellent health. You once saved her life. Now she's given you a son. Let it be enough."

Carlo's words penetrated through to his soul. What was the Spanish proverb? *Be careful for what you wish, for you just might get it.*

Vincenzo stood there helpless as hot tears trickled down his cheeks.

"Good morning, honey."

"Dad—"

"I'm here."

"This is a different room."

"That's right. You're in a different hospital. You were transported in an ambulance after the delivery."

"I'm so thankful it's over and Vincenzo has his baby."

"Yes. He's overjoyed. I'll turn on the TV so you can see for yourself." Carlo raised the head of the bed a little for her to see without straining.

Abby saw the flash, "breaking news," at the bottom of the screen. "For those of you who are just waking up, this is indeed a morning like none other in the history of the world. There's a new royal heir to the throne of Arancia. Last night at six-fifteen p.m., a baby boy was born to Crown Prince Vincenzo and the deceased Princess Michelina Cavelli by a gestational surrogate mother who we are told is doing well. The new young prince has been named Maximilliano Guilio Cavelli Di Laurentis."

Vincenzo...

"The seven-pound prince is twenty-two inches long."

"Max is beautiful, Daddy." The tears just kept flowing. "He'll be tall and handsome like Vincenzo!"

"According to the proud grandparents, their majesties King Guilio Di Laurentis and Queen Bianca Cavelli of Gemelli, the baby is the image of both royal families.

"We're outside the hospital now, awaiting the appearance of Prince Vincenzo, who will be taking his son home to the royal palace any minute. A nanny is already standing by with a team to ease Prince Vincenzo into this new role of fatherhood.

"Yes. The doors are opening. Here comes the new father holding his son. We've been told he's not going to make a statement, but he's holding up the baby so everyone can see before he gets in the royal limousine."

Darling. Abby sobbed in joy and anguish.

"This must be a bittersweet moment for him without Princess Michelina at his side. But rumor has it that sometime next year the king will be stepping down and the Principality of

Arancia will see another wedding and the coronation of Prince Vincenzo."

Abby was dying for Vincenzo, who was being forced to face this. "I can't stand the media, Dad. Couldn't they let him enjoy this one sacred moment he and Michelina had planned for without bringing up the future?"

"Speculation is the nature of that particular beast. But we can be thankful that for this opening announcement, they played down your part in all this. For such forbearance we can thank the king, who told me to tell you that you have his undying gratitude."

Abby's hungry eyes watched the limo as it pulled away from the hospital escorted by security. The roar of the ecstatic crowds filled the streets. Her father shut off the TV.

She lay there, numb. "It's the end of the fairy tale." Abby looked at him. "I can't bear it. I love him, Dad, but he's gone out of my life."

He grasped her hands. "I'm proud to be your father. You laid down your life for him and Michelina and he has his prize. Now it's time for you to close the cover of that scrapbook and start to live your own life."

"You knew about that?"

Her father just smiled. He wasn't the head of palace security for nothing.

Abby brushed the tears off her face. "I gave it to him months ago when he told me he didn't want to be king. I wanted him to look through it and see all his accomplishments."

Her father's eyes grew suspiciously bright. "You've been his helpmate all along and it obviously did the trick."

She kissed his hand. "Thank you for keeping him away as long as you could. I didn't want him to have to go through any more grief, not after losing Michelina. Forgive me for yelling at you at the apartment?"

"That's when I knew you meant business. As it so happens, I agreed with you, but a man should be at the bedside of the woman who's giving birth to his baby. Evidently Angelina thought so, too. She's the one who told him to get to the hospital quick."

"Bless her. I needed him there."

"Of course you did."

"Lucky for me I was blessed to have you there, too, Daddy."

"Someday you'll get married to a very lucky man, who will be there when the time comes for your own child to be born. I look forward to that day."

Abby loved her father, but he could have no conception of how she felt. Vincenzo was the great love of her life. There would never be anyone else and she would never have a baby of her own. But she'd had this one and had been watched over by Vincenzo every second of the whole experience.

Through the years she would watch Max in secret, because he was her son and Vincenzo's as surely as the sun ruled the day and the moon the night. No one could ever take that away from her.

"Honey? The nurse has brought your breakfast." He wheeled over the bed table so they could eat together. "Do you feel like eating?"

Abby felt too much pain and was too drugged

to have an appetite yet, but to please her father she reached for the juice.

"We haven't talked about you for a long time." She smiled at him. "I want to know the real reason you decided to step down and move back to Rhode Island. Is there a woman in the picture you haven't told me about? I hope there is."

He drank his coffee. "There has been one, but it was complicated, so I never talked about it."

"You can talk to me about it now." Because if there wasn't, then it meant she and her father had both been cursed in this life to love only one person. Now that she'd lost Vincenzo, both she and her dad would be destined to live out the rest of their lives with memories.

"Can't you guess? There's only been one woman in my life besides your mom. It's been you."

"Don't tease me."

"I'm not."

She frowned. "Then why did you decide you wanted to leave Arancia?"

"Because I could see the hold Vincenzo has had on you. Otherwise you would never have offered yourself as a surrogate. If you hope to get on with your life, it has to be away from here."

Abby lowered her head. "I'm afraid he'll always have a hold on me."

"That's my fear, too. It's why we're getting out of Arancia the moment you're ready to travel."

CHAPTER TEN

VINCENZO HAD SUMMONED Angelina to his apartment as soon as he'd returned to the palace with his son. He'd spent time examining Max from head to toe. After feeding him the way the nurse had showed him, and changing his diaper, Vincenzo gave Max to the nanny, who put him to bed in the nursery down the hall. Now there was no time to lose.

"Tell me what you know of Abby's whereabouts, Angelina."

"I can't, Your Highness. Please don't ask me. I've been sworn to secrecy."

"By whom? Carlo?"

"No."

"The king?"

"No."

"Abby?"

She nodded.

He knew it!

"Tell me which hospital they took her to."

Angelina squeezed her eyes tightly. "I don't dare."

"All right. I'm going to name every hospital in Arancia." He knew them all and served on their boards. "All you have to do is wink when I say the right one. That way you never said a word."

"She'll hate me forever."

"Abby doesn't have a hateful bone in her body. She carried my son for nine months and gave me the greatest gift a man could have. Surely you wouldn't deny me the right to tell her thank you in person."

"But she's trying to honor her contract."

"Contract be damned! She's fulfilled it be- yond my wildest dreams. If another person had done for you what she's done for me, wouldn't you want to thank them?"

"Yes, but—"

"But nothing. That may have been the rule when Michelina and I signed on with her, but the baby has arrived. There's no more contract.

You're free of any obligation. What if I tell you I won't approach her in the hospital?"

After more silence he said, "I'll wait until she leaves. Surely that isn't asking too much. I swear on my mother's grave she'll never know you told me anything."

Still more silence. He started naming hospitals while holding his breath at the same time. Halfway down the list she winked. His body sagged with relief. San Marco Hospital, five miles away in Lanz. Near the airport and several luxury hotels. It all fit.

"Bless you, Angelina. One day soon you'll know my gratitude with a bonus that will set you up for life."

As she rushed away, he phoned his personal driver. *"Giovanni?"*

"Congratulations on your son, Your Highness."

"Thank you. I need you to perform a special service for me immediately."

"Anything."

He'd been doing a lot of undercover services

for Vincenzo since the pregnancy. "I hope you mean that. My red sportscar is yours if you do as I say."

His driver laughed. Giovanni came from a poor family.

"You think I'm kidding?"

"You are serious?"

"Do as I say and you'll find out. I want you to round up all your cousins *pronto* and have them drive to San Marco Hospital in Lanz. Signorina Loretto is there recovering from the delivery. She's being watched by her father's security people. Fortunately they don't know your cousins.

"I want them to cover all the hospital exits leading outside. She'll be leaving there by private limousine. I suspect it will happen by this evening if not sooner. When your cousins spot the limousine, they'll follow and report to you when her limo reaches its destination, which I believe will be a hotel, possibly the Splendido or the Moreno. Then you'll phone me and drive me there. Any questions?"

"No, Your Highness. You can count on me."

"There's a healthy bonus waiting for each of them. My life depends on your finding her, Giovanni."

"Capisci."

Vincenzo hung up and hurried down to the nursery to spend time with his precious son before his father and sister arrived. He had to stop Abby from leaving the country. If she got away, he'd track her down, but it would be much more difficult with the baby. He wanted her here. *Now!*

He played with his baby and took pictures with his phone. While the family took turns inspecting the new arrival, he took a catnap. Bianca and Valentino would be flying in tomorrow morning.

At five in the afternoon, his phone rang. He saw the caller ID and picked up. "Giovanni?"

"We've done as you asked. She was driven to the Moreno under heavy guard."

"I'll be right down." After telling Marcello his life wouldn't be worth living if he told anyone where Vincenzo was going, he put on sunglasses and rushed down to the limo in a Hawaiian shirt, khaki shorts, sandals and a droopy straw hat.

Giovanni took off like a rocket. "You look like all the rich American businessmen walking around the gardens. No one would recognize you in a million years, Your Highness," he said through the speaker.

He bit down hard. "If I can make it to her room before someone stops me, it won't matter."

Carlo had made Abby comfortable on the couch in their hotel suite. This would be their home for a few more days before they left the country. The painkillers they'd given her were working.

"Is there anything you want, honey?"

She kept watching the news on TV to see Vincenzo and the baby. "Would you mind picking up a few magazines for me to look at?"

"I'll get them. Anything else?"

"A bag of dark chocolate bocci balls and a pack of cashews." She'd been starving for foods she couldn't eat during the pregnancy. They wouldn't take away her depression, but she needed to give in to her cravings for some sweets or she'd never make it through the next few days.

"I'll have to go down the street for those."

"Dad—take your time. I'm fine and you need a break. Thank you."

A few minutes after Abby's father left, there was a knock on the door. "Room service."

She hadn't ordered anything, but maybe her father had. "Come in."

"Grazie, Signorina."

Abby knew that deep male voice and started to tremble. She turned her head in his direction, afraid she was hallucinating on the medicine. The sight she saw was so incredible, she burst into laughter and couldn't stop.

Vincenzo walked around the couch to stand in front of her. "What do you think?" he asked with a grin, showing those gorgeous white teeth in that gorgeous smile. "Would you recognize me on the street?"

She shook her head. "Take off the glasses." She was still laughing.

He flung them away and hunkered down next to her. His eyes blazed black fire. "Do you know me now?"

Her heart flew to her throat. "Wh-what are you doing here? How did you find me?"

"You'd be surprised what I had to go through. Giovanni's my man when I need him. Did you really think I was going to let you go?"

Tears stung her eyes. "Don't do this, Vincenzo."

"Do what? Come to see the woman who has changed my entire life?"

She looked away. "You have a beautiful son now. We had an agreement."

"I hate agreements when they don't give me the advantage."

Abby couldn't help chuckling, despite her chaotic emotions. "Is he wonderful?"

"I'll let you decide." He pulled out his cell phone to show her the roll of pictures.

"Oh, Vincenzo—he's adorable!"

He put the phone on the floor. "So are you. I love you, heart and soul, Abby."

The next thing she knew, his hands slid to her shoulders and he covered her mouth with his own. The driving force of his kiss pressed her head back against the pillow. His hunger was so shocking in its intensity a moan escaped her throat in surrender.

A dam had burst as they drank deeper and deeper, but Abby's need for him was out of control. She had no thought of holding back. She couldn't.

"For all my sins, I love and want you to the depth of my being, Vincenzo, but you already know that, don't you? I tried not to love you, but it didn't work. Everything your sister said to me that day in the drawing room was true."

His lips roved with increased urgency over her features and down the side of her neck to her throat. "I fell for you years ago when you almost drowned, but I would never admit it to myself because a relationship with you was out of the question. No matter how hard I tried not to think about you, you were there, everywhere I looked. You're in my blood, *bellissima*."

They kissed back and forth, each one growing more passionate. "It seems like I've been waiting for this all my life," she admitted when he let her up for breath.

"We've paid the price for our forbearance, but that time is over. I'm not letting you go."

Abby groaned aloud and tore her lips from his. "I can't stay in Arancia."

"There's no such word in my vocabulary. Not anymore."

"She's right, Vincenzo."

Her father had just walked in the hotel room, carrying some bags. Her breath caught as she eyed him over Vincenzo's shoulder.

"Carlo." He pressed another kiss to her mouth and got to his feet. "I'm glad you're here so I can ask your permission to marry Abby. She's my heart's blood."

Rarely in her life had she seen her father look defeated. He put the bags on the table and stared at the two of them.

"I don't want an affair with her. I want her for my wife. Since you and I met when I was eighteen, you can't say you don't know me well enough."

Her father moved closer. "That's certainly true." He looked at Abby. "Is this what you want?"

"Yes." Her answer was loud and instantaneous.

Vincenzo reached for her hand and squeezed it. "I have no idea if the parliament will allow my marriage to a commoner and still let me remain crown prince. If not, then I don't intend to be in line for the crown and my sister will take over when the time comes."

"Are you prepared to be the targets of malicious gossip for the rest of your lives?"

"If necessary we'll move to the States with our son. He *is* our son. One way or another, she and I have been in communication whether in person or skyping. Max is every bit a part of her as he is of me and Michelina."

Carlo swallowed hard.

"I love Abby the way you loved your wife. The state you were in when you lost her altered my view of what a real marriage could be. If Abby leaves me, I'll be as lost as you were."

Vincenzo was speaking to her father's heart. She could tell he'd gotten to him.

"I know the king's feelings on the subject, Vincenzo. He was hoping you would follow after him."

"I was hoping I would fall in love with Michelina. But we don't always get what we hope for. If it's any consolation, Gianna always wished she'd been born a boy so she'd be first in line. She'll make a great ruler when the day comes."

"Are you two prepared to face the wrath of your mother-in-law?"

Vincenzo glanced at Abby. "We'll deal with her. When she sees Michelina's likeness in Max, her heart will melt. I know she'll secretly be full of gratitude to Abby, who put her life on the line for Michelina and me to give her a grandson."

"Dad?" Abby's eyes pleaded with him. "What do you think Mom would say if she were here?"

He let out a strange sound. "She always did say it was sinful that Prince Vincenzo had been born with every physical trait and virtue any red-blooded woman could want. Since she loved films so much, she would probably say yours is one of the greatest love stories of this generation and should be made into a movie. Then she'd give you her blessing, as I give you mine."

"Carlo..."

Vincenzo was as moved as Abby, who broke down weeping. He finally cleared his throat. "I want her to move back into the palace tonight in her old room until we're married. Max needs his mother tonight, not a nanny or a nurse."

"In that case a quiet, private marriage in the palace chapel needs to be arranged within a week or two. Just as soon as you've talked to the king."

"I don't want you to take that job back in Rhode Island, Dad."

He broke into a happy smile. "Since I'm going to be a grandpa, I guess I'm stuck here."

"That'll be music to my father's ears." Vincenzo put his hands on his hips. "Do you feel well enough for the trip back to the palace now?" he asked Abby.

She stared at him. "I feel so wonderful, I'm floating. I want to see our baby."

"Do what you need to do while I help your father get everything packed up. Then we'll go out to my limo for the drive back."

"I'll just run to the restroom and grab my purse." Except she walked slowly and looked back at Vincenzo. "I'm waddling like a goose."

His laughter resonated off the walls.

In a few minutes she was ready. When she came back into the room, she found he'd donned his hat and sunglasses. When she thought he would take hold of her hand, he picked her up like a bride, as if she were weightless.

"You and I have done things differently than most of the world. Now we're about to cross the threshold the other way."

"And me looking such a mess." She didn't have on makeup and her hair hung loose, without being brushed.

"You're the most beautiful sight I ever saw in my life." He gave her a husband's kiss, hot with desire.

"So are you," she murmured, resting her head against his shoulder.

Her father opened the door. "The men have the hallway closed off to the exit. Let's go."

After leaving his stunned father and sister in the king's private living room, where he'd announced he was getting married, Vincenzo headed for the nursery. He found Max sleeping and gathered him in his arms. The nanny left for Abby's apartment, wheeling the bassinet on its rollers down the hall. He followed and carried his son through the corridors of the palace. One day their little boy would run on these marble floors.

The staff all wanted to steal a look at Max, but Vincenzo was careful not to let them get too close. Dr. DeLuca had warned him to keep Max away from people during the next few weeks. He found Abby on top of the bed with her eyes closed. After fifteen hours in labor, she had to be exhausted. She was wearing a blue night-gown and robe and had fastened her gilt hair back at the nape.

Their nanny put the bassinet with everything they would need to one side of the queen-size bed and left the apartment. Since both were asleep, Vincenzo put the baby in the little crib on his back. Then he got on the other side of the bed and lay down facing Abby.

It felt so marvelous to put his arm around her. He'd wanted to do this on the yacht and had been aching for her ever since. While she slept he studied the exquisite oval mold of her face. Her lips had the most luscious curve. He had to pinch himself this was really happening. To have his heart's desire like this was all he could ever ask of life.

Abby sighed and started to turn, but must have felt the weight of Vincenzo's arm. Her eyes flickered open.

"Good evening, Sleeping Beauty." The famous fairy-tale character had nothing on his bride-to-be.

Her eyes looked dazed. "How long have you been here?"

"Just a little while. *Viene qui tesoro.*" She *was* his darling.

He pulled her closer and began kissing her. Abby's response was more thrilling than anything he'd ever dreamed about the two of them. Vincenzo had promised himself to be careful with her. The kind of intimacy he longed for wouldn't happen until her six-week checkup, but he already knew she was an exciting lover.

They didn't need words right now. There'd been enough words expressed to last months, years. The kind of rapture they derived from each other had to come from touch, from her fragrance, from the sounds of her breathing when she grew excited, from the way she fit in his arms as if she were made for him. She was the fire, giving off life-giving warmth. He couldn't get close enough.

In the throes of ecstasy, he heard newborn

sounds coming from the other side of the bed. He planted one more kiss to her throat. "Someone's waking up and wants to meet his mama."

With reluctance, he rolled away from her and walked around to the crib. "I've got a surprise for you, *piccolo,* but let's change your diaper first." Practice made perfect.

Abby sat up higher on the bed, her eyes glued to the baby he placed in her arms. "Oh—" she crooned, bending over to kiss his face. "You darling little thing. You're already a kicker, aren't you? I've been feeling your father's legs for several months and thought you had to be a boy. Are you hungry? Is that why you're getting all worked up?" Her soft laughter thrilled Vincenzo's heart.

He handed her a bottle. She knew what to do. It fascinated him to watch her feed him as if she'd been doing it every day. A mother's instinct. Deep down he knew she'd been thinking about it from the moment she found out she was pregnant.

"Give him about two ounces, then burp him. Here's a cloth."

What took him awhile to learn she seemed to know instinctively. When she raised Max to her shoulder, their little boy cooperated and they both chuckled. She raised a beaming face to him. "I'm too happy."

"I know what you mean," he murmured emotionally.

"I hope you realize I wanted to talk about the baby for the whole nine months, but I didn't dare."

"You think I don't understand?" He sat down on the side of the bed next to her and watched a miracle happening before his eyes. "We'll take care of Max all night and feed him every time he wakes up."

"I can't wait to bathe him in the morning. I want to examine every square inch of him."

Vincenzo leaned over to kiss her irresistible mouth. "Once the doctor gives you the go-ahead, I'm going to do the same thing to *you*."

Blood rushed to her cheeks. "Darling—"

* * *

Abby had just put the baby down in the nursery when her cell phone rang. She hurried out of the room, clutching her robe around her, and slipped back in the bedroom she shared with her husband to answer it. "Carolena!"

"You're a sly one."

Her heart pounded in anxiety. "I was just going to call you. I guess the news is officially out."

"Out? It's alive and has gone around the world. I've got the Arancian morning news in front of my eyes. I quote, 'Crown Prince Vincenzo Di Laurentis marries commoner surrogate mother Abigail Sanderson Loretto in private chapel ceremony with only members of the immediate family in attendance. The question of the prince stepping down is still being debated by the parliament.

'The twenty-eight-year-old first-time mother, an American citizen born in Rhode Island, attained Arancian citizenship six years ago. At present she's an *avvocata* with Faustino, Ruggeri, Duomo and Tonelli.

'Her father, Carlo Antonio Loretto, a native of Arancia who served in the Arancian Embassy in Washington, D.C., for a time, is chief of security for the royal palace. His American-born wife, Holly Sanderson Loretto, is deceased due to a tragic sailboat accident eleven years ago on the Mediterranean.

'Prince Maximilliano Guilio Cavelli Di Laurentis, the son of deceased Princess Michelina Agostino Cavelli of the Kingdom of Gemelli, is second in line to the throne.

'The spokesman for the palace reports that Prince Vincenzo's wife and child are doing well.'"

Abby gripped the phone tighter. "This day had to come, the one the three of us talked about a year ago, when I first met with Michelina and Vincenzo. But I didn't know then that she would die." Her voice throbbed before breaking down in tears.

"I know this is hard, Abby, but you might

take heart in the fact that the paper didn't do a hatchet job on you and your husband. They presented the facts without making judgments, something that is so rare in the media world, I found myself blinking."

"That's because of the publisher's long-standing friendship with the king. I shudder to think what the other newspapers have printed."

"I haven't read anything else except the story in one magazine. Do you remember the one after Michelina's death that said The Prince of Every Woman's Dreams in Mourning?"

"Yes." She'd never forget.

"The quote now reads, 'Hopeful royal women around the world in mourning over prince's marriage to American beauty.'"

Abby groaned. "The truth is, that magazine would have been writing about me if he'd decided to marry Princess Odile."

"But he didn't!" Carolena cried out ecstatically. "Listen to this article from that same magazine. 'Enrico Rozzo, a sailor in the coast guard who was at the scene of the terrible death of

Holly Loretto, the mother of then seventeen-year-old Abigail Loretto, said, "Prince Vincenzo thought nothing of his own life when he went in search of Signorina Loretto during the fierce storm. He found her body floating lifeless in a grotto and brought her back to life. His bravery, skill and quick thinking will never be forgotten by the coast guard.'"

Abby's body froze. "How did they get hold of that story?"

"How do they always do it? It's a glowing testimonial to your husband, Abby. He's well loved."

"I know." *By me most of all.* She was blinded by tears, still euphoric after knowing Vincenzo's possession for the first time.

"Just think—he married *you* under threat of losing the throne. Talk about Helen of Troy!"

A chuckle escaped despite Abby's angst. "Will you stop?"

"I always thought you were the most romantic person I ever knew. After what you went through to get that baby here, no one deserves a happier ending more than you."

"I'm not looking very romantic right now." She wiped her eyes. "At my six-week checkup yesterday morning, the doctor told me I'm fifteen pounds overweight. I won't be able to wear that gorgeous yellow dress for at least two months! I look like an albatross!" Carolena's laughter came through the phone.

"A stunning albatross," Vincenzo whispered, sliding his arms around her from behind. She hadn't heard him come in. He was in his robe.

At his touch Abby could hardly swallow, let alone think. "Carolena? Forgive me. I have to go, but I promise to call you soon. You've got to come to the palace and see the baby."

"I can't wait!"

He was kissing the side of her neck, so she couldn't talk.

"Your time is coming."

"When the moon turns blue."

"Carolena, you're being ridiculous."

"A presto."

The second Abby clicked off, Vincenzo took the phone and tossed it onto one of the velvet chairs. He pivoted her around and crushed her against him. "Do you have any idea how wonderful it is to walk into a room, any room, day or night, and know I can do anything I want to you?"

She clung fiercely to him, burying her face in his hair. "I found out how wonderful it was yesterday after you brought me home from my checkup." Heat filled her body as she remembered their lovemaking. She'd responded to him with an abandon that would have been embarrassing if he hadn't been such an insatiable lover. They'd cried out their love for each other over and over during the rapture-filled hours of the night.

"I told the nanny we'd look in on the baby tonight, but for the next eight hours, we're not to be disturbed unless there's an emergency."

"We've got eight hours?" Her voice shook.

His smile looked devilish; he rubbed her arms as a prelude to making love. "What's the matter? It *is* our honeymoon. Are you scared to be alone with me already?"

Her heart was racing. "Maybe."

"Innamorata—" He looked crushed. "Why would you say that?"

She tried to ease away from him, but he wouldn't let her. "I guess it's because the news has gone public about us at last. I don't want you to regret marrying me. What if the parliament votes for you to step down? It's all because of me."

He let out a deep sigh. "Obviously you need more convincing that I've done exactly what I wanted. Whether I become king one day or not means nothing to me without your love to get me through this life." He kissed her mouth. "Sit on the bed. There's something I want to show you."

While she did his bidding, he pulled the scrapbook from one of his dresser drawers. "I've been busy filling the pages that hadn't been used yet. Take a good long look, and then never again accuse me of regretting the decision I've made."

With trembling hands she turned to the place where she'd put her last entry. On the opposite page were the two ultrasound pictures of the baby. Beneath them was a news clipping of her on the steps of the courthouse the day she'd won the case for Signor Giordano. A quiet gasp escaped her throat as she turned the pages.

Someone had taken pictures of her coming and going from the palace. Pictures of her on the funicular, at the restaurant, the swimming pool, the yacht, the church where she'd worn the hat, pictures on the screen while they'd Skyped. But she cried out when she saw a close-up of herself at the opera. The photo had caught her in a moment of abject grief at the thought of a permanent separation from Vincenzo.

He'd always found a way to her...

Abby could hardly breathe for the love enveloping her. "Darling—" She put the album on the bedside table and turned in his arms. He pulled her on top of him.

"You're the love of my life and the mother of my child. How can you doubt it?" he asked in that low, velvety voice she felt travel through her body like lava, igniting fires everywhere it went.

"I don't doubt you, sweet prince," she whispered against his lips. "I just want you to know I'll never take this precious love for granted."

"I'm glad to hear it. Now love me, Abby. I need you desperately. Never stop," he cried.

As if she could.

* * * * *

Mills & Boon® Large Print

September 2014

0814 Rom LP

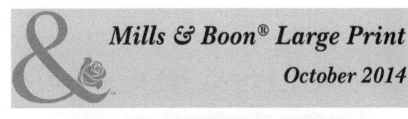

Mills & Boon® Large Print
October 2014

RAVELLI'S DEFIANT BRIDE
Lynne Graham

WHEN DA SILVA BREAKS THE RULES
Abby Green

THE HEARTBREAKER PRINCE
Kim Lawrence

THE MAN SHE CAN'T FORGET
Maggie Cox

A QUESTION OF HONOUR
Kate Walker

WHAT THE GREEK CAN'T RESIST
Maya Blake

AN HEIR TO BIND THEM
Dani Collins

BECOMING THE PRINCE'S WIFE
Rebecca Winters

NINE MONTHS TO CHANGE HIS LIFE
Marion Lennox

TAMING HER ITALIAN BOSS
Fiona Harper

SUMMER WITH THE MILLIONAIRE
Jessica Gilmore

914 Rom LP

MILLS & BOON®

Why shop at millsandboon.co.uk?

Each year, thousands of romance readers find their perfect read at millsandboon.co.uk. That's because we're passionate about bringing you the very best romantic fiction. Here are some of the advantages of shopping at www.millsandboon.co.uk:

* **Get new books first**—you'll be able to buy your favourite books one month before they hit the shops

* **Get exclusive discounts**—you'll also be able to buy our specially created monthly collections, with up to 50% off the RRP

* **Find your favourite authors**—latest news, interviews and new releases for all your favourite authors and series on our website, plus ideas for what to try next

* **Join in**—once you've bought your favourite books, don't forget to register with us to rate, review and join in the discussions

Visit **www.millsandboon.co.uk**
for all this and more today!